TRUE COLORS

Dixie DuBois

A KISMET™ Romance

METEOR PUBLISHING CORPORATION
Bensalem, Pennsylvania

To Joy Rich, a selfless friend.
   Vickie

To my grandmother, Ruth Zeigler, who taught me
about "true love."
   Dixie

DIXIE DUBOIS

"Wanted: person with a working knowledge of the
English language (or at least a good typewriter).
Object: contemporary romance novels." This classi-
fied ad, and a shared love for writing and romance,
brought Vickie DuBois and Dixie Gaspard together,
and "Dixie DuBois" was born. Both authors live in
the heart of *Cajun country* in south Louisiana. They
are currently working on their second novel together.

ONE

Nikki Colomb swerved her green compact into Archer Oil's unpaved parking lot, slinging clamshells against the metal-sided structure. Startled by the noise, a red-winged blackbird rose with an angry cry from his perch in a nearby willow and flew toward the vast saltwater marshes beyond the screen of chinaball and chicken trees on the far bank of the Intracoastal Canal. On this Saturday morning the dispatcher's truck was the only other vehicle in the Archer Oil field office parking area. A helicopter sat on the heli pad a little distance away, beyond the orange survival capsules and huge tanks waiting to be transported to oil platforms off the Louisiana coast.

"Where is he?" Nikki demanded, leaning over George Breaux's desk.

"Who?" the young dispatcher asked uneasily.

"You know who." He knew. She didn't. The Archer Oil Company representative whose curt phone call had wakened her this morning had only informed her that the Colomb's small oilfield contracting firm was fired. He hadn't even explained why.

If she hadn't been quite so angry, she might have noticed the grim line of George's normally smiling mouth, and the way his hand trembled as he set down his coffee cup.

"It's no good, Nikki. You can't go in there," he said, glancing at the door to the inner office.

"In here?" she asked, moving to the door and through it before George could deter her. She pressed the lock as she swung it shut behind her. She'd had the thirty-minute drive to stew over that daybreak phone call, and she was angrier than ever. She wasn't about to take the chance that George might evict her before she could find some way to regain their contract—or, failing that, to tell off the arrogant baboon who'd called her!

As George ineffectually rattled the doorknob, hissing for her to come back, Nikki squared her shoulders and looked around. She was familiar with this office. She'd had a few difficult talks here with Archer's Vermilion district supervisor, Randolph Grimes. Like most oil company field offices, it was plain to the point of austerity. The formica-topped conference table, vinyl covered chairs, and a battery of metal filing cabinets were the main features.

Nikki wasn't sure just what she'd been expecting. What she found was paperwork—mounds of it—stacked atop every available surface. The filing cabinets that lined the wall stood with drawers open and empty. There were only two people in the room, although it seemed unlikely that just two people could be responsible for this mess.

The call had come from a man. It was a man Nikki wanted. Her violet gaze pinned one, his shoes propped atop a heavily laden desk as he applied a cordless razor to a strong, suntanned jaw. The shoes, she decided, were about size twelve. Yes, the voice on the phone might have rumbled from that broad chest. This had to be the man she wanted.

The other occupant of the room, a svelte blonde in a crisp white linen suit, took immediate exception to Nikki's presence. She rose from behind a portable computer workstation linked to a telephone modem. A professional frown drew her perfect sable brows together. "I'm sorry," the secretary began, in a tone that revealed that she wasn't sorry in the least, "But— Miss!" The last as Nikki deftly sidestepped her professional blocking maneuver and zeroed in on the man behind the large footwear.

Nikki planted herself before the desk, hands on the hips of her coveralls, and her eyes glittering dangerously. But the penetrating gray eyes that met hers made her forget momentarily what she was angry about. They were silver-gray, deepset beneath straight dark brows, and she found she couldn't look away.

His face was planes and angles, bronzed by the sun. His blackbird-wing hair was short, thick, and pushed back from an intelligent forehead. Beneath his straight nose was a mustache trimmed to the exact width of his upper lip. It spread slightly as he smiled. The underlip was sensuously squared at the corners.

It was some seconds before she noticed a tugging at her arm. Looking down, she found the secretary's exquisitely manicured hand curled around her forearm. Nikki eyed it as if it was a dead fish.

"I'm sorry!" the secretary said reproachfully. "Mr. Archer cannot be dis—"

"It's all right, Svenson," Julian Archer cut in, a whisper of amusement in his rich voice. "I'll see this young lady."

The name Archer hadn't been lost on her. She tried

to gather her wits as she turned and watched the secretary's exit. What could the high muckity-muck of Archer Oil be doing in this Louisiana backwater?

And why had he canceled their contract?

Nikki turned back to face Julian Archer and mentally caught her breath. She now recognized him from his pictures in Archer Oil's newsletter. Those photographs had only hinted at the man.

Archer rose. He was tall; a head taller than Nikki's five-foot-seven. She absently noted that her eyes were level with the dark hair curling at the opening of his shirt. His coat and tie had been discarded on the back of the desk chair, and the wheat-colored shirt covering his wide shoulders emphasized his deep tan. The sleeves were rolled back, revealing tautly-muscled forearms. Dark suit pants sheathed his slim hips and long, powerful-looking legs.

She was usually indifferent to a man's looks, assessing physical appeal with interested detachment. But something about this man was different. He had a compelling presence; an attraction that ran through her like a warm breeze. He was disturbing.

Nikki, suddenly aware that she'd been openly appraising the man, dragged her eyes guiltily back to his face. His chiseled mouth curved in a mocking smile.

"Oh! Do sit back down!" Nikki snapped. To make matters worse, she felt a blush rising to her cheeks. This was the arrogant baboon she'd come here to find, she reminded herself. The man who'd just consigned Colomb Contractors to bankruptcy! "It's one thing to glower down at someone, but it's quite difficult to glower up at someone effectively!"

Dark brows lifted. Humor glinted in the silver-gray eyes like sunlight dappling a clear, fast-running brook. "My dear, if I glowered at you like that—" He suited action to words as his gaze leisurely swept over her, lingering where her breasts thrust against the sturdy fabric of her work clothes, and the very feminine curve of her hips. "You might misinterpret what I was thinking, Miss . . . ?"

"Ms.," Nikki supplied dryly. Snatching her hard hat from her head, she reversed it and thumped it down on the desk between them. COLOMB CONTRACTORS was neatly lettered on the back. "Colomb. Nicole Colomb."

The atmosphere cooled.

Archer's eyes narrowed. He flipped open an attaché case and began to sort through the manila folders on the desk, stacking some of them inside it, beside a compact cellular phone. "Then I haven't anything more to say, Ms. Col—"

"Well, I have a great deal to say!" Nikki interrupted him as her temper boiled over. "Maybe you're used to casually sweeping people aside, but I'm not. When the people who work for Colomb Contractors ask me why they're standing in the unemployment line, I'd like to have something to tell them. What will it be, Archer? 'Sorry guys, but after ten years at Indian Point, Archer just dropped our contract without one word of explanation'?"

"This is why, Ms. Colomb." Archer indicated the mountains of paperwork with a sweep of his hand. Some of it—well tests, shipping reports, daily reports— was in Nikki's own tight scrawl. "I don't like being taken for a fool to the tune of a million and a half dollars!"

Nikki stared at him and pushed trembling fingers through her thick mahogany hair. She hadn't the faintest idea what he was talking about. "If you're referring to lost revenues due to down time," Nikki snapped. "I won't be held responsible for your shoddy, second-rate equipment! If you've read these at all, you'd know that I've detailed the cause of each shut-in—usually equipment failure. I've also listed problems that are about to happen and made recommendations to prevent them. Grimes doesn't want to spend a dime out there. He and I have been 'round and 'round about this already. I'm not going to jury-rig everything, or leave the panelboard pegged out, bypassing the safety switches. If he recommended that you drop our contract because of it, then . . . then . . . Oh, garbage!'' The last as Nikki realized just who she was telling off. *That's it, idiot!* she congratulated herself. *Alienate the man even more—if possible!*

Stuffing fists into the deep pockets of her coveralls, she turned away and took out her frustration on a metal folding chair with a kick that sent it skittering across the linoleum tile. It thumped over with a satisfying twang! If Nikki had dared to look at the man behind her, she would have found a puzzled expression on his dark, handsome face. She didn't look; she was too busy trying to get her emotions under control. Her sustaining anger had fled, and an overriding sense of failure pressed down on her. She had to lose her temper, didn't she! What would she tell Pop Colomb?

"Ms. Colomb?"

"Yes?" She turned and her gaze was captured by Archer's penetrating gray eyes.

Those eyes! A portrait took shape in her mind. Yes, the planes and angles of his face would lend themselves easily to canvas, but the essence of the man glinted in those eyes: one minute warm and smoky, the next flat and hard as moonstones. Now, filled with storm clouds of changing emotions. Always alive with the keen intelligence behind them. They would be as difficult to capture on canvas as they would be essential to the portrait. She could almost feel the brush in her hand.

Surprised at the direction her thoughts had taken, Nikki blinked and forced her attention back to what Archer was saying.

"Are you saying that you and Grimes didn't get along?"

Nikki grimaced. Another nail in Colomb's coffin. She despised Randolph Grimes, but there was little point in lying about it. She knew instinctively that this man would see through a lie. "No," she answered woodenly. Then her head swung up as she realized that he had spoken of Grimes in the past tense. "What do you mean, Didn't? Where is Grimes?"

Archer ignored her questions. Moving to the window, he rested his arms on the chest-high sill and watched the progress of a big river tug pushing a full load of barges up the wide Intracoastal Canal.

"When did you take charge of Colomb Contractors?" he asked without turning. "I remember meeting an older man a few years back. Heavyset. Thick gray hair. He had a son who was a dynamite nose guard for LSU."

"That would be my father-in-law. It's still his company, but he's no longer in good health."

There was a slight hesitation. "You're married, then."

"A widow. The nose guard. An accident."

"Sorry." Archer turned back to her, his dark brows raised slightly. Speculatively.

Nikki nodded acceptance of his condolences. It had been a long time since anyone had offered their sympathy. The same length of time since she'd felt like a hypocrite as she made some polite reply. She wasn't sorry that Bob was dead—no, that wasn't true. She couldn't wish him, or anyone, dead. But she wasn't sorry that she was no longer his wife. Nikki drew in a deep breath and asked, "Where is Grimes, Archer? What's this all about?"

"Grimes, I would say, is on a plane to Rio, a million-plus under his arm."

Nikki's eyes rounded and her violet gaze swept the paper-filled room in sudden understanding. These were the invoices, work orders, and other daily records of what had happened at Archer's leases over the last few months. "Embezzlement?"

"The figure is still just an estimate. How much he skimmed in good-old-fashioned kickbacks is anybody's guess." Nikki noticed his emphasis on the word kickbacks. As he outlined the details, she also noticed that he watched her closely—for her reactions?

Knowing Grimes, it didn't surprise her when Archer told her how several local supply companies and oilfield service companies had padded their invoices and kicked back part of the profits. But the Archer supervisor had become greedy. He'd set up his own dummy corporations and billed Archer for work never done and equipment never received. The regional supervisor in Houston had eventually become suspicious.

When Archer had finished, Nikki asked with a frown, "So how does that explain why Julian Archer, in the flesh, comes down from his black glass tower?"

"Because," he informed her tautly, "Grimes was a family friend. He was with my father when Dad was just starting out.When he looked me up a few years ago for a job, I made a place for him. When the VP from accounting got the report questioning certain expenses, he turned it over to me and I came here myself, hoping that it wasn't true. But someone in

Houston must have tipped off Grimes—he'd already bolted.''

"And you called every local company that you thought was involved?" Nikki asked in growing disbelief.

"I don't like being taken."

"And you believe that Colomb Contractors was in with him!" Nikki exclaimed.

"I haven't made any formal charges." His tone said, *not yet.*

"Well, we weren't! We wouldn't do anything like that! How dare you assume that we would!"

At that instant, the secretary reappeared. She announced that the helicopter would be checked out and ready to take off in a few minutes.

Nikki felt a surge of panic as the engine whined to life on the helipad outside. "At least give me the opportunity to prove that we weren't involved." There was a note of pleading in her voice that she hated.

"And how do you propose to do that?" Archer asked.

"I . . . I don't know just yet," Nikki confessed, and she felt the heat rise in her cheeks at his mocking smile. "But I will!"

He chuckled as he shrugged his wide shoulders into the dark blue coat of his business suit. "You're either very honest, or very clever. I think I'd like to find out which. I'll give you until Friday to make your case, lady."

"Thank you!"

Nikki's sudden smile snagged his gaze. "Then I'll be back to take you out to dinner."

Her smile died. "I . . ." She caught the refusal that sprang to her lips and looked warily up into those dangerous gray eyes. When had he gotten so close?

"Yes or no will do." Archer's smile was mocking as the silence lengthened.

Nikki drew herself up to full height. "I'm waiting for you to tell me that your decision about the contract doesn't hinge on whether I agree to go . . ." *Or agree to anything else, for that matter,* Nikki added silently.

"Are you?" His slight smile deepened, and his teeth flashed white. He straightened his tie with a few deft flicks of his long, square-tipped fingers. The drone of the helicopter increased.

"I see," Nikki murmured. What choice did she have? A strong instinct for self-preservation warned her that she wasn't equipped to deal with a man like Julian Archer. An awareness of his compelling masculinity already hummed along her nerves like a low-voltage current.

"You're not afraid, are you?"

"Of course not!" Nikki answered too quickly. That current increased by several hundred kilocycles as he raised her chin with his forefinger and gazed into her violet eyes. "Just wondering . . . why you'd want to go out with me, is all," she sputtered.

Archer laughed softly. "Because you interest me."

She found herself nodding acceptance, surprised at how much the prospect excited her—almost as much as it frightened her.

"Good. I'll call you." Archer picked up his attaché case and left.

Nikki bolted upright in bed, her lungs gulping air. Her wide-open eyes saw muddy river water rushing in through the shattered windshield of Bob's pickup. She was trapped, pinned beneath Bob's weight as the truck sank. Then, slowly, the nightmare faded, and she recognized the familiar shapes of her white wicker furniture in the early light.

Nikki sucked in a deep breath, released it slowly, and hugged her knees tightly to her chest, rocking back and forth. The horror of the nightmare had left a hot, sick feeling at the back of her throat. It always did.

Damn, when would it stop happening? *When?* Bob had died more than five years ago, but she was dreaming about the accident more and more often.

Nikki pushed her hair away from her damp forehead and glanced at the clock radio on her bedside table: 5:38. She'd never get back to sleep now. And she needed the rest. Worry about the business with Archer had kept her awake most of the night.

A few minutes later she sat in the peacock-style wicker rocker, wrapped against the early morning chill in her fuzzy pink robe. Cradling a mug of hot cocoa, Nikki drew in a deep breath. It came out as a sigh. The familiar surroundings of her bedroom comforted her.

When she had been searching for a new apartment a few weeks after Bob's death, the wall of French windows in this bedroom, which opened onto a veranda overlooking the garden, the high ceilings, and the heart-of-pine floors had captured Nikki's imagination. She'd decorated the room herself, hanging the powder-blue wallpaper with its French ribbon design. She'd sewn a comforter, bedruffle, and priscilla curtains of white eyelet. She'd brought nothing except her clothes and a few personal items from the apartment she had shared with Bob.

Through the open French windows of her apartment, the second floor of an old Victorian house, she watched as the Louisiana morning dawned bright and clear. Beneath a moss-hung live oak, the Vermilion River blushed pink in the early light. A tug boat chugged past and gave three sharp blasts of its airhorn, warning the drawbridge keeper a little farther upriver of its approach. Its wake broke like a miniature surf, lapping at the narcissus bordering the back garden.

Nikki sipped her cocoa, then smiled as she heard her landlady in the garden below. Mrs. Deshotels, a habitually early riser, was chatting in Cajun French with her cat, Mignon, about the fushsia azaleas the elderly lady was clipping.

Nikki's smile faded as her gaze moved to the open sketchbook on the bedside table. The unfinished pastel crayon portrait of her landlady's cat taunted her silently. The perspective of the picture was excellent. The use of color and texture was good. But it had no life. No spark. Neither had her four earlier efforts, which now lay crumpled around the wastebasket beside the table. They had gone from bad to worse.

Nikki put her cocoa aside and slid the sketch pad onto her lap, studying the flaws in the picture. It used to come so easy to her. Pictures had seemed to spring to life at the ends of her fingers as she'd sketched without conscious thought. But since Bob's death . . .

She ripped the picture from the pad, crushed it, and pitched it toward the French windows. She picked up the burnt sienna pastel from the table, then changed her mind and chose the umber instead. But as she began to draw, Julian Archer's face, the sound of his voice, filled her head. Frustrated, she tossed the pastel back into the box and dropped the sketch pad to the floor.

Nikki tried to clear her mind as the bells of St. Mary Magdeline a few blocks away began to call six o'clock mass. It was obviously tension that was affecting her sleep. This week had been a disaster even before Archer had fired them. Tuesday, a switcher had called to report an expensive meter stolen from Sunland Oil's Bancker Plantation field. Worse, the thieves had left the broken line dumping crude. By the time their operator found the damage, the containment levy around the well was about to overflow, which would have spilled crude oil into the marsh. Then, Friday afternoon, the saltwater pumps of Archer Oil's Nunez well had gone out. It had been well past ten that night by the time she'd gotten parts "hotshotted" out to the rural location and the well back in operation.

She wasn't sure how she had come to supervise Colomb Contractors. She had never consciously desired a position where half the problems in the Vermilion Parish oilfields landed in her lap. She'd just inherited it. Pop had relied on Bob a great deal after Bob had quit college, turning more and more of the business over to him. Then, after Bob's death, Pop had suffered a heart attack. Nikki took leave from college and pitched in, doing what she could to help maintain the business. At first that had been as go-between from Pop's hospital bed to the field. When, a few months later, Pop fell victim to a second heart attack, she found herself working full time.

Pop had recovered enough to go to the office for a few hours on most days, but he'd never again be able to shoulder all the responsibilities.

Someone would have to take care of this problem with Archer Oil, and it couldn't be Pop. She'd have to dig through the office records herself. Then she'd keep that date with Julian Archer . . . but only to show him proof that he was wrong about Colomb Contractors.

TWO

It was unseasonably warm. With one of the sudden changes common to the weather of southern Louisiana, the cool of spring had vanished. The wind had fallen to a faint breeze and the sun bore down. Rising over the warm Gulf waters to the south, beyond Southwest Pass, the first thunderheads of the season mushroomed. Beneath them, the growing humidity hung in a steamy, iridescent haze.

With a graceful movement of her hand, Nikki lifted her shining mahogany hair from her neck. The breeze slipped beneath her collar, cooling the perspiration along her spine.

Her gaze skimmed over the grayish waters of Vermilion Bay. A seagull lifted off a tripod of pilings and flapped away over the "Christmas tree," the strange looking cluster of valves and pipes where an oil well emerged from the water. The bird dove with a cry and skimmed a small fish from a school of mullet swimming near the surface.

The eight wells, which supplied Archer Oil's Indian Point Lease, weren't located on the tank battery, but in the waters surrounding it. Pilings driven deep into the muddy bottom and topped with navigation lights protected each of the Christmas trees. The produce from the wells went by flow lines to the main platform, where the oil, water, and natural gas were separated. Archer hired Colomb Contractors to oversee these processes.

Nikki moved along the catwalk between the tops of two huge oil storage tanks. Above the heavy chugging of the natural gas compressor on the far side of the platform, an improbable duck hunting story floated up to her from the roustabout crew on the lower deck. They had spent the day cleaning the fire tube of the heater-treater and were now catching a five-minute break. Shutting in the wells and breaking into the huge vessel had been quite a job, but they had finished in good time. The fact that it was Friday may have inspired the men to speed, Nikki thought wryly.

The duck hunting broke up as the gang-pusher ordered the men to clean up the mess on the deck and to put away the tools. Nikki dropped the gauge line into a tank, noted the depth, and added the reading to a tally book she took from her hip pocket.

It had been a hectic week. Much to her surprise, Julian Archer had wasted no time in acting on the information in her reports. The new supervisor at the district office had been out to Indian Point three times already, and Nikki had been bringing roustabout crews out daily to tackle the problems. Did that mean Archer trusted her a little? she wondered. She hoped so, for she had no idea at this point how to convince him that Colomb Contractors wasn't involved with Grimes.

"What a mess!" Nikki muttered.

She wished that Pop Colomb had been a little easier to approach on the matter. He'd become so angry and upset when she'd tried to talk to him about what was happening, she'd been concerned that he'd have another heart attack. She'd found herself telling him that she was sure she could straighten everything out. Now, he was relying on her—but what was she going to do?

She was acutely aware that she'd be seeing Julian Archer tonight. He'd be expecting some answers. She closed her eyes for an instant and wavered with fatigue. She'd been up most of last night going through the company's financial records for the past year—without any conclusive results. She had hoped to have tangible proof to show Archer. She wanted to keep this evening strictly business. But from the speculative look in the man's gray eyes . . .

Agreeing to go out with Archer had been crazy. Insane. She had dated since Bob's death, but those evenings had been companionable and relaxed. This one promised to be a male-female jousting match; not at all what she was prepared for. Perhaps if her life had taken a little different turn, she might have learned how to laugh and flirt and play those little games the society girls played—girls that attracted men like Julian Archer. She'd never been any good at it.

Nikki finished her rounds and started back toward the "doghouse." Kent Miller, the gang-pusher, surprised her as he stepped out from behind a separator vessel. Nikki had the uncomfortable feeling that he'd been watching for her.

"Hi," Nikki gave him a bright but impersonal smile. "You guys ready to go to the beach? I can meet you at the boat in ten minutes."

"Yeah. That'll be fine," he casually dismissed business, blocking her way between two huge tanks when she would have breezed past. "Nikki, there's grease on your chin, girl."

"That's a new type of skin cream," she quipped. She had learned that the best way to get along in this predominantly male environment was to make no excuses for her femininity. She pulled off her work glove and wiped at the smudge, smearing it.

"You already got nice skin." Kent smiled. His Cajun accent lent a lilting cadence to his words. "There's a trail ride out to Prairie Greig this weekend. They'll be kickin' things off tonight with a *fais-dodo*. I sure would like it if you'd go with me," he said, moving closer.

"It's very nice of you to ask, Kent, but—"

"It ain't nice at all," he told her disgustedly, as if he'd been half-prepared for a refusal. "You'd have fun. I'd have fun. We'd dance a little two-step, drink a little draft—Nikki, you and me, we could pass a good time, *cher*."

"No. Thank you," she told him firmly but kindly.

"Look, Nikki girl, you young, *cher*!" His Cajun accent thickened with his agitation. "What you gonna do? You gonna stay married to a dead man all your life? *Cher bon Dieu*!" Shaking his head expressively, he stalked away.

Startled, Nikki stared after him. Is that what everyone thought? she wondered, stunned. Did they all assume that she was still in love with Bob? The irony of it almost made her laugh, even as her eyes grew moist.

"You might have told him that you have plans," offered a deep voice behind her.

Nikki's head jerked around. Julian Archer was leaning casually against a flow line. Her violet eyes widened in disbelief. "Where did *you* come from?" she demanded, flicking a glance at the empty gray water off the side of the platform.

"I didn't walk," he assured her. "I took one of the company boats from the dock in Intracoastal City. I can tell you're thrilled to see me."

"You just hid there, eavesdropping, didn't you?" Nikki snapped.

"I was fascinated."

"I'm delighted!"

"My business in Baton Rouge finished early, so I decided to come out and look things over," Archer said, offering no apologies, as he watched a bead of perspiration slip down her graceful neck and cross the sun-pinked skin exposed by the vee of her collar, to disappear into a shadowy cleft below. "Actually, I wanted to see you at work."

"Many women work in the oilfield nowadays, Mr. Archer," Nikki said. "Now, if you don't mind, I'd like to get away from the heat of these vessels before I fry."

He captured her hand as she tried to brush past him. "How did you come to work here, by the way?" he asked, smiling. Nikki rather wished that he wouldn't. At close range, it had the power to take her breath away a little. "And my name is Julian."

He took the red cloth riding above her back pocket, pulled it out, and wiped at the smudge on her chin. The action, and the faint, clean scent of his skin made her acutely self-conscious of her own grit and grime.

"Thank you!" She snatched the rag back, ignoring his question.

"Show me around?" he asked.

Nikki gave him a tour of the platform. At the heater-treater they found Jo Jo Schexnader and 'Tee Floyd Bergeron, her fellow operators. After making introductions, she slipped away to the doghouse.

Inside the tiny building, Nikki heated water in an

electric kettle and made a cup of tea, then gathered together her daily paperwork.

"That looks good," 'Tee Floyd said as he and Jo Jo joined her a few minutes later. Archer hesitated in the doorway, surveying the eight-by-ten room. It contained a small table and a few metal folding chairs. One wall was filled with cabinets and bins for the various meter charts. Static crackled from a two-way radio on a shelf.

"Oh, no! Not that tea," said 'Tee Floyd, pulling a comic face as he realized that it wasn't coffee she was sipping. "Haven't you ever heard of good Cajun coffee, girl?" he scolded.

Nikki laughed. "I kept the water hot, so you could drip coffee if you like."

"Now you talkin'." 'Tee Floyd took a diminutive porcelain drip pot down from a shelf and began spooning a generous amount of coffee into it as he urged Archer to pull up a chair.

Jo Jo explained, as 'Tee Floyd added water to the pot a few drops at a time, that the secret to good coffee was that it must be dripped slowly, and the coffee never, never allowed to boil.

"You'll join us, won't you, Mr. Archer?" 'Tee Floyd asked. "You ain't gonna take tea like this *Anglais* here? I don't think I'm ever gonna make her into a good Frenchman!"

"I beg your pardon," Nikki laughed, picking up their playful mood. "My maiden name was Duval. I was French long before I came to Vermilion Parish." The teasing was a welcome diversion. It almost distracted her from the disturbing weight of Archer's gaze.

"Duval, eh?" 'Tee Floyd seemed to consider this as a revelation. "Well, maybe there's some hope for you yet. But I know what your problem is, *cher*. That's

New Orlean's French. It's kinda watered down. Now, good Cajun blood, it's like this coffee.''

"You gonna take some with us, ain't you, Mr. Archer?'' Jo Jo asked, taking down demitasses, sugar, and creamer. "It ain't every day I get to take coffee with the head honcho of Archer Oil.''

Archer eyed the tiny pot doubtfully. "If you're certain there is enough.''

For about thirty people, Nikki speculated privately. She smiled benignly as he refused sugar and creamer. She waited for the result.

"Rich,'' Archer murmured at some length. She couldn't keep the merriment from her eyes as they met his.

"I'm certain Ms. Colomb would enjoy some of this,'' . . . *paint remover,* he finished to himself.

"Oh, no!'' Nikki laughed. "I never drink 'Tee Floyd's coffee in the afternoon—not unless I want to stay awake all week! Now, if you'll excuse me, Mr. Archer, ladies''—to 'Tee Floyd and Jo Jo—"I really must go and bring the roustabouts back to the landing.'' Nikki looked forward to escaping Archer's presence—at least for a little while. He was to pick her up for dinner at eight. A shower, some makeup, and feminine clothes would give her more confidence in handling this man.

"Don't hurry off,'' Archer told her. She didn't like his imperious tone.

"I really must!'' Nikki insisted sweetly. "They probably would have left without me by now, if I didn't have the keys to the boat in my pocket.''

'Tee Floyd and Jo Jo roared with laughter.

"What's so funny?'' she demanded.

"*Mais cher,*'' Jo Jo laughed heartily, "that's just what they did!''

"I don't understand.'' Nikki looked from one co-

TRUE COLORS / 27

worker's face to the other. Even Archer was smiling. *And I have a feeling that I won't like the explanation!* she added to herself.

"I sent them back on the *Miss Lou*. I didn't think that you'd mind talking me back to Intracoastal."

Nikki gave the tall man a dark look. "I see no way I could object," she told him drily.

A short time later Julian Archer was lounging in a passenger seat of Colomb's crewboat, his attention absorbed by a sheaf of papers as he spoke quietly into a microcassette recorder, both of which he'd taken out of his attaché case. Nikki settled herself deeper in the captain's chair and wished for bad weather. His presence made her vaguely uncomfortable, and she certainly hadn't expected him to ignore her.

The water was uncooperative. Instead of becoming choppy, the bay was changing from wrinkled blue crepe to the silvery satin of afternoon calm beneath a sky the same hue. In the west, the setting sun touched the water with flames of orange and peach and gilded the clouds.

The boat, powerful twin-diesel engines droning, practically drove itself. Nikki grew heavy-lidded as the day's tension was lulled from her body. She had to force herself to remain alert.

"Do you mind if I smoke?" Archer's deep voice snapped Nikki's attention back to her passenger. She shook her head, and he placed a thin cheroot between his teeth. She dragged her eyes back to the water before her as the spicy-sweet aroma mixed with the salty air.

"You were right," Archer said after a while. Nikki arched an inquiring brow. "It will be difficult for your men to find other jobs. They're both in their mid-fifties, and 'Tee Floyd is illiterate, isn't he?"

She stared at him for an instant. She'd known that the man was perceptive, but how had he found that out? " 'Tee Floyd has a third-grade education. Jo Jo made it through the seventh. But Floyd knows your lease like the back of his hand and Jo Jo is a whiz at anything mechanical. They're both very reliable employees," Nikki told him stiffly.

Julian Archer's dark brows rose. "I didn't say they weren't."

"You implied it."

"No. You inferred it."

She was acutely aware that he'd said "Will be unemployed," and not "Would be," as if there were no doubt that they would lose the contract. "How did you know?" she wondered aloud.

"Before going into the doghouse, Floyd went into the compressor building to check something and I tagged along. I asked him some questions about the compressor log on the clipboard there. I had wondered why every scrap of paper I'd seen from the Indian Point Lease was written in the same indecipherable handwriting—yours, I assume. By the way, why did you sneak away to the doghouse back there? Were you planning to leave without me?"

"I didn't know at that time that you wished to charter this boat. The fee is three-fifty, by the way."

"Put it on your monthly bill to Houston."

"I will."

"I've never spent that much to buy a woman's company before," Julian mused aloud.

Nikki kept her attention fixed forward, letting the remark slip over her head and out the open window.

He wasn't sure what it was about Nikki Colomb that made him more perverse than usual. Or why he'd looked forward all week to being with her. She wasn't even that pretty—at least not in the way most of the women he dated were pretty. Strangely, her unusual looks made her even more attractive than many women he'd known with model-perfect faces. She had wonderful cheekbones—almost too prominent. Her nose wasn't some childish button of a thing, but firmly sculpted, with the hint of a bump near the bridge. Her chin was too pointed, but that didn't seem to matter; it suited her. Like those unusual eyes. A velvety blue-violet. They were turned downward at the outer corners and shadowed by thickly curling lashes. There were inward shadows, too. What those shadows meant, he could only guess. Her mouth . . . ah, well, that was perfect, her underlip full, soft, moist looking. Very kissable.

Perhaps it was that air of innocence wrapped about her like a cloak which provoked him. He wanted to peel it back, confront the woman underneath. She certainly must have known what Grimes was up to. And if she had been running Colomb Contractors, she had to be up to her pretty neck in it.

"I meant what I said about 'Tee Floyd and Jo Jo being good workers," she reiterated.

"I'm sure that you did."

She turned and studied him, as if judging the amount of sympathy and understanding he was capable of. He found the look irritated him. He wasn't some sort of monster. If anything, he'd been more than reasonable.

"They, and a great many others like them, are victims of prejudice, Archer. They grew up before the oil beneath these marshes opened this area to industry and influences outside their native French-Acadian culture. Most people made their living by hunting and trapping or farming. They raised their kids. Tended their crops. Went to mass. And spoke French. In most cases, exclusively French. Then the government built schools which taught only in English. Kids started school, not knowing a word of English, and were ridiculed and punished

or even spanked if they were caught speaking French—
even at recess or lunch. It's no wonder that many of
their generation resisted education.

"Of course, the area is no longer isolated. Suc-
ceeding generations have become Americanized. Now,
many of the kids speak only English. They have a problem communicating with their own grandparents."

Archer nodded in comprehension. But his mouth
twitched with a supressed smile. "Raised their kids and
tended their crops and went to mass. Sober stuff for the
people who coined the phrase *'Laissez Les Bon Temps
Roulet.'* "

Nikki pulled back on the throttles as another boat
approached them in the Four Mile Cutoff, the canal
leading from the bay to the Intracoastal. The big alumi-
num hull came off the step and began to plow through
the brackish water. "Oh, look!" She pointed ahead as
the boat nosed over the other vessel's wake. In a side
slip where a barge had once drilled unsuccessfully, a
great blue heron stood poised in the shallows, arrow-
shaped head held perfectly still, long neck folded,
patiently waiting for his supper to swim by.

Archer rose and leaned over her shoulder. "Beautiful," he murmured, barely glancing at the bird, his
gaze resting lightly on her profile.

"This area has an abundance of wildlife."

"You'll have to show me."

Her head swung around at the unmistakable inflection
in his voice, but she bit back a retort as Archer blinked
in mock innocence. She was not going to let the man
bait her!

As the boat neared the dock, he took up a position
on the bow. Nikki expertly maneuvered the boat into a
narrow dock space, using the twin propellers to move

the craft laterally. Most of the dock was taken up by a stacked drilling barge belonging to Archer Oil.

Flinging a two-inch line like a lasso, Julian successfully circled a piling above the bulkhead. He tied the other end off on a cleat. He trotted down the gunwale and repeated the process at the stern.

"That wuz shore sum fancy ropin', cowpoke," Nikki drawled as she joined him on deck. He took the case and jacket she held out to him.

"Aw, shucks. Twaren't nuttin', ma'am. I've had lots of practice." Nikki smiled at his exaggerated Texas twang. The sight made him feel curiously warm. His gaze shifted to the rig and the feeling cooled.

"You're a sailor, then," she asked.

"Not really. I have a catamaran hidden away at my grandmother's house in Bay St. Louis, but I never seem to have time to take it out. I learned to rope the summer my brother, Frank, decided that he was going to make us the junior team-roping champions at the Texas State Rodeo. I guess I must have roped a million hay bales while he was teaching me."

"And were you? Champions, I mean?"

"Frank was. Bull dogging. I just had to try my hand at bareback riding. I was in the hospital getting a broken collar bone set when Frank took the prize for calf-roping. . . ."

Nikki smiled. "I always wanted a brother. It must have been nice."

He jumped to the dock and extended a hand and helped her across. Nikki suddenly found herself trapped on the outermost edge of the wharf, her back to the water, her nose almost touching Archer's muscular chest. She dared to tilt her head back and found him studying her closely. Something about the way he was looking at her made her skin feel tight. The feeling continued after he'd stepped aside.

"Yes, it was nice having a brother." She was puzzled by the cold, forbidding tone of his voice. "Although Frank probably had the worst of it. He not only had to put up with a pesky younger brother, but I think our father was grooming him to take over the company from the day he could walk. Dad mostly left me to my own devices.

"The summer before Frank was to enter Princeton, Dad put him to work on a rig like that one," indicating the stacking drilling barge. "Dad wanted him to learn the business from the ground up, like he had. Frank was on his own. No one knew he was an Archer. The consultant on the job had a deal going with some fly-by-night tool company. He was pocketing a healthy kickback in exchange for renting their tools. Worn-out junk hardly fit for scrap iron!" He ground out the words, his eyes stabbing hers. "The first week—the very first week out, Nikki—the brake failed. Frank lost an arm." He grasped her upper arms. She could see the pain beneath the dark anger in his face. "Now do you understand why I have no patience with people who sell out?"

It was a demand. She nodded mutely, sensing that there was something he wanted from her but unable to understand what it was. "I'm sorry," she said softly. "What happened to him? I've never heard his name in connection with Archer Oil."

Julian's eyes closed against the sympathy he saw in her eyes. Damn, she was good! He could almost believe . . . He released her and looked out on the water. "Frank isn't connected with it. He has a ranch in Montana where he's raising kids and prize-winning charolais cattle. The funny thing is that he never really wanted to be saddled with the corporation. He just didn't know quite how to get out of it. After the accident, he told Dad where to get off and began doing the things he wanted to do.''

"Leaving you as heir to the oil barony."

Archer looked deeply into those wide blue-violet eyes. She seemed only curious. In fact, she didn't seem to be hiding anything at all. Maybe, she *was* an excellent actress.

"Did you resent that?" Nikki asked as his gaze began to make her feel a little breathless.

"Resent it? I don't think I've ever thought about it before . . . No, business is an interesting game," he told her. Then with a wicked smile, his eyes dropping to her mouth, "I've always enjoyed games."

She ignored the comment. "With the price of crude where it is, your rig won't be stacked long." She glanced at the drilling barge. It seemed a safer subject.

"Good times or bad, there's always profit to be made somewhere. I've been told some dock owners are collecting small fortunes for dock space."

The innuendo was unmistakable. "We aren't!" Nikki's anger flared. "We'd be pretty stupid to overcharge your company for dock space when we're contracted by you. That would be biting the hand that feeds us."

"So what do you charge?"

"Nothing, as far as I know. Think of it as a perk."

"You're sure?"

She tried to read his expression, but his eyes were screened by thick lashes. What was he getting at? Or did he simply enjoy being obnoxious? She decided it was the latter. "Certain. I spent a great deal of last night going through our company records. There was no record of collecting any dock fees.

"Now, may I offer you a lift to the Archer office?"

Suddenly, she couldn't wait to get away from this man—if only for a few hours. Having to endure that probing gaze made her irritable. If he kept this up, how would she ever get through this evening? "If you have no moral objections to being seen in a compact?"

"I prefer gas-guzzlers. A matter of principal, you understand." A half-smile curved Archer's mouth. "I flew down in the helicopter. I'm afraid that you're stuck with me for the evening." Archer reached out and twirled a mahogany curl around his finger, its burnished highlights glinting in the sun. He watched in amusement as several emotions passed across Nikki's face. The play ended with a saccharine smile.

"Wonderful! Then let's not waste time. We'll go straight to my apartment," she purred. His dark brows rose with interest. "And I'll show you that Colomb wasn't involved with Grimes in any illicit way!" she finished abruptly. "I'm sure you're as anxious as I to finish our business."

"But then I've never minded mixing business and pleasure," Archer said.

She turned her back on his infuriating chuckle and, taking out her keys, tried to unlock her car. After three attempts, a large hand closed over hers and removed the keys from her fingers. Archer opened her car door and mockingly bowed her in. As he got in on the passenger's side, Nikki found suddenly that *she* had a strong objection to compacts. They caused people to sit far too close together. In fact, Archer's wide shoulders seemed to take up most of the room in the front seat. He could lean over more toward the door!

She was keenly aware of the warmth of his body and of her arm brushing his as she shifted gears. By the time she pulled up in front of her apartment, her hands were trembling.

Julian Archer seemed to unfold as he got out of the small car. Nikki was privately pleased to see him flex his shoulders, as if he'd grown cramped. He looked around with interest. The house was a slate blue with cobalt shutters. An unbelievable amount of cream gingerbread trimmed the wide porches on both upper and lower floors. A live oak, wider than it was tall, dominated the yard. Some of its thick black limbs dipped low enough for one to sit on them.

The limbs overhead left deep pools of shadow over the yard and the outside stairs. Archer took her elbow and guided her up. Nikki didn't even attempt the lock. She silently gave him her keys. What was it about this man that made her fingers feel so clumsy?

"Please, go into the parlor and make yourself at home," she offered with inborn southern courtesy. Then she escaped into her postage-stamp sized kitchen.

"Parlor?"

"What else would you call a room with sixteen-inch baseboards?" she called back.

Tossing her hard hat on the counter, Nikki leaned against the cool metal of the refrigerator and drew in a steadying breath. She could hear him making use of her phone to order a rental car. Good. It seemed that she could still feel the warm pressure of his shoulder against hers. She had no wish to be that close again. Damn the man! She didn't like the effect Julian Archer had on her. Whenever she was around him, she found herself out of her depth; caught up in games that made her lose control of her emotions.

Nikki caught sight of her be-grimed appearance in the mirror surface of the toaster, and almost laughed aloud. Right now, he could hardly find her attractive.

A shower, she thought, pouring herself a glass of chablis. There was little more she wanted of life at this moment than to crawl beneath the stinging needles of her shower. Other than Julian Archer to concede that Colomb Contractors was innocent of any wrongdoing and then take his wide shoulders and silver eyes away, leaving her in peace.

Carrying a tray of fruit and cheese in one hand and a bucket of ice with the other, Nikki joined him in the parlor a few minutes later. It was a pleasant room. The loose cushioned furniture looked comfortable and inviting. Several brass planters held lush green plants. On the low Chinese table before the sofa, a variety of magazines hinted at the diverse interests of their owner. A tumble of chintz cushions in rose and mauve and moss green filled the window seat built into the huge bay window. The same color theme was carried on in the striped wallpaper. Area rugs added pools of color to the polished floor. One wall—the wall given a northern exposure by the big bay windows—wasn't hung with paper, but painted eggshell white. On it were displayed several paintings of various sizes and themes.

It was before this wall that Julian Archer stood. His expression was one of rapt wonder. As Nikki approached, he turned to look at her, then his gaze shifted to the nearest painting, as if he seriously doubted that the person standing before him and the Nicole Duval who had signed the painting were one and the same.

The painting was a large acrylic, a street scene from a New Orleans *Mardi Gras*. The masquers in brittle-colored costumes were forever caught in frenzied revelry against a night-dark sky. The street scene made his pulse throb to the beat of New Orleans jazz, while above the scene, tucked away in the night shadows, a cinnamon-haired child gazed down through the wrought-iron bars of a balcony. Her expression, half cynical, half wanting-to-believe, caught at his heart.

Julian tore his eyes away as if he couldn't bear to look too closely. Nikki Colomb had intrigued him. Now he felt as if he had almost shamefully invaded her privacy. As if he had truly looked into her soul.

"What in the hell are you doing in the oilfield?"

THREE

Nikki was taken aback. "What are you talking about?"

"*This* is what I'm talking about!" He made a sweeping gesture at the paintings displayed on the wall. "Why are you wasting your time out there, when you should be painting full-time?"

She looked away from his intense gaze. "I happen to like doing a *real* job and making a *real* contribution to life, instead of playing with paint."

"Operating an oil lease is an invaluable contribution to mankind." Archer's sarcasm stung.

"The world needs fuel," she snapped hotly.

"Almost anyone could be trained to operate a lease. Only *you* can do this. You've got something special."

"I don't paint anymore," Nikki said, trying to make her tone light, as if it wasn't important. It was. It was terribly important. For so many years, in the gloomy museum of a house on St. Charles where she'd grown up, her pencils and watercolors and pastels had been magical keys which helped her escape. As she had grown, her love of art had grown, too, until sometimes she had seemed possessed by a driving need to capture life on paper or canvas as it paraded by the windows. Yes, it was terribly important. And far too personal to discuss. She had no intention of trying. "I don't paint anymore," she said again, half to herself, unwilling to meet his probing gaze. Those eyes always seemed to invade her privacy. Why did he make her feel as if she had to explain everything? It was really none of his business, anyway.

Realizing that she still held the ice bucket that she'd brought in from the kitchen, she set it down on the rattan bar cart. Lead crystal decanters, rocks glasses and tumblers were arranged on the glass shelves. "Here's Scotch. There's bourbon"—indicating which decanter was which with a flick of her hand—"and there's wine and sodas in the refrigerator. Our company records are in that box beside the sofa. Now, if you'll excuse me, I'd like to shower and change. I'm told I have a date."

Archer caught her shoulders as she started to turn away. The contact was electric. His eyes, like molten silver, bore into her stormy purple ones. But if Nikki's were storm clouds, Archer's were lightning. They streaked through her, causing a frisson along her spine. She caught her breath as his gaze moved to her mouth.

His strong hands relaxed their hold and slipped down her arms, softly caressing, like the first sensuous breezes which came before a powerful storm. His eyes became smoky with promise as he studied the contours of her face. Nikki knew that she wasn't beautiful—still in dirty coveralls, her whole being faded from working all day in the heat of the platform, she felt a great deal *less* than beautiful.

What she couldn't know was how compelling Julian Archer found her. Or, this last week, how often he'd remembered a pair of violet eyes. Like her paintings, there was something about this woman which drew his eyes back.

Beneath his hands, Nikki trembled. She was confused by the feelings that poured through her; the wave of desire that became a physical ache; alarm that it somehow mattered to her what he thought. She wanted to fall against him and feel her breasts crushed against his deep chest. An instinct for self-preservation cried out in her. She wanted to turn and run.

But she stood immobilized under his gaze.

His hand slipped to her throat. His thumb beneath the point of her chin tilted her face upward as his mouth came down. To Nikki, the descent seemed to take eons. Anticipation raced along her nerve endings, so that when his warm, firm lips found hers, she almost cried out.

No one had ever affected her this way before and it frightened her. But as he molded her to him, she couldn't think beyond the pleasure of his mouth moving over hers. She couldn't move. She was barely able to breathe. And when he broke the contact, there was disappointment.

After a moment, Nikki felt him draw in a deep breath and expel it slowly.

Archer kissed her lightly on the forehead and turned away. "Go get your shower. I think I'll take that drink."

"Damn," Nikki muttered as she closed the door to her bedroom. She leaned heavily against it and closed her eyes, suddenly unbearably tired. Almost immediately the memory of Archer's mouth moving over hers, his fingers sliding down her spine and drawing her against his hard thighs replayed in her imagination, sending shafts of heat from the center of her outward.

Her eyes flew open. "Damn!" Nikki couldn't understand what the man did to her. She had wanted to keep it just business, but he had insisted on provoking her. Now her incomprehensible attraction to the man had betrayed her.

She'd never thought of herself as a passionate person. Bob had excited her when they were dating. Marriage, well, had been disappointing. So much so that after Bob's death, she'd never considered another serious relationship.

Nikki forced herself to face the truth as she took her time showering and dressing. He'd probably never seen a woman in work boots and hard hat. She was a novelty to him. His appetite for rich society girls had probably become jaded and he was amusing himself with something new. He'd lose interest as soon as the new wore off.

And since forewarned was forearmed, Nikki decided there was no reason not to go out and have fun. Was there?

Nikki chose a simple shirtwaist dress that flattered her femininity and she took her time applying her makeup and enameling her nails. When she was finished dressing, she checked her appearance in the wicker framed cheval glass and smiled. If it was tomboyishness which appealed to him, Archer would soon discover that she didn't qualify, she thought with satisfaction. She touched her favorite perfume to her wrists and to the pulse beating beneath the point of her jaw, then joined him in the parlor.

Archer stood as she entered, his eyes sweeping from the toes of her evening sandals to where her skirt whispered about slender calves to her thin waist and upward to her breasts, high, firm, and tip-tilted. Her eyes were made even more dramatic by subtle shadow and mascara. The light reflecting off the French blue silk of her dress changed their purple quality to an enigmatic lavender.

He smiled in appreciation.

"I knew that you were a beautiful woman, Nikki," he growled softly. "I just didn't know how much those coveralls were hiding."

"Thank you," Nikki murmured, amazed that she could say anything at all after his jarring appraisal. Well, she had wanted to show Archer that she was female, hadn't she? Smart move. She felt as if she'd just shown some dark predatory cat that she was *filet mignon*.

She retreated into the kitchen and dug the chablis out of the refrigerator. She tossed down a fortifying glass and poured another. Then, on impulse, she brought the bottle back into the parlor. Archer didn't seem to notice her return. His dark head was bent toward a column of figures as he rapidly fed them into a calculator, his attention completely absorbed.

Nikki was thrown off balance by the change. Then, with a flash of insight, she understood the power of concentration which allowed him to focus his attention completely on whatever he was doing, tuning out distraction.

Hadn't she once possessed that ability—or rather, been possessed by it in the form of a consuming need to put brush from palette to canvas? It had been a process which demanded everything from her; a way to escape, to shut the rest of the world out.

Her talent had been art. Julian Archer's was business.

Nikki curled into a Queen Anne-style wing chair and placed the wine bottle on a side table. "Are you almost finished," she asked, anxious for the moment when he would admit that he'd been wrong about Colomb Contractors. It would be a weight lifted from her mind.

"Almost." Archer totaled the column, then sat back. His eyes were opaque, unreadable. "Precisely what in this—" he indicated the business records, which he had formed into neat stacks "—did you want me to see?"

"I . . . I wanted you . . ." A frown etched little lines above the bridge of her nose and Nikki looked down, swirling the wine in her glass for an instant before raising her gaze back to his. "I don't know," she confessed reluctantly. "I'm unfamiliar with this sort of thing. I work in the field, while Pop handles the business. I stayed up most of last night trying to sort through this, but all those figures just confused me. But then I'm not an accountant."

"Then why exactly are you showing these to me?" he asked.

"Because you won't be confused. I mean you aren't, are you?" He shook his head slightly. She went on, "I knew that when you went through our financial records for the last six months, you'd *see* that Colomb is blameless."

Nikki could tell nothing by his expression.

Archer lit a cheroot. His gaze followed the smoke he exhaled, then moved to the powerful paintings and caught there for an instant before shifting back to the woman who had created them. He had thought her diamond hard beneath her soft exterior. But the person who portrayed life with such insight and sensitivity had to be genuine. Could it be that his suspicions were wrong; that she was as honest as she seemed? He had to know for certain.

Nikki was warmed by the spark of wonder in the look he gave her. The after-image stayed with her, even though his expression rapidly changed into what Nikki thought must be his business face: very cold and unapproachable.

It was a mask carved by boardroom in-fighting, by fending off unfriendly takeover attempts by the ever-circling corporate sharks. He had skyrocketed Archer Oil so high, so fast, that it was no longer viable prey for most of that hungry school. Although, at his direction, Archer Oil had gobbled up a great many lesser concerns on its way up and absorbed them into its corporate body.

It was the face of a minor deity, she realized. His day-to-day decisions affected the lives of thousands: the employees of Archer Oil and its subsidiary companies, and the families of those employees. Their well-being was directly related to the well-being of Archer Oil and the capabilities of the man in charge.

He was capable of accepting that ultimate responsibility. And for an instant, before the mask of corporate CEO had settled into place, she had seen that Julian Archer was in awe of her.

It was a heady thought. And one Nikki quickly rejected as impossible. *My dear, you must be drunk,* she told herself wryly. And she realized with a small bubble of surprise that it was true. Of course, it was simply done. Take one-half bottle of wine, one empty stomach, one exhausted body, and one weak mind. Add wine to stomach, and the rest took care of itself. Women engaged in mad fantasies about being held in adoration by a deity. About being held by a deity. About—

Whoa! Just because you've drunk too much wine is no excuse to get carried away! she chided herself.

"What if I told you that these records don't show Colomb to be innocent; that there are discrepancies, but that I'm willing to overlook them in exchange for one of your paintings?" Archer asked, his tone emotionless.

If she had conspired with Grimes, she would jump at his offer. He hoped she wouldn't.

Nikki put her hand to her mouth and stifled a giggle, but couldn't keep a smile from blooming beneath her fingers. "You can't bait me, Julian Archer. I know you wouldn't do that."

Archer's dark brows rose.

"You wouldn't lie to get what you wanted," she explained calmly as she studied him over the top of her glass. As she went on, it was the artist in her which spoke. "You could be ruthless. Yes, I can see that in you. And I think you could pursue what you want singlemindedly. But you would never lie to take what you want. You play by the rules. And, as I remember how you looked in Grimes's office, I'd say that you get mad as hell at anyone who doesn't! If you want a painting, though, you can have one. I'm not even sure why I keep them."

Julian Archer considered the toe of his shoe in silence for a moment. Nikki had the impression some strong emotion passed behind his mask. It was gone before she could name it. "You seem to have thought about me a great deal," he said at length. As he lifted his dark head, his gray eyes caught her and drew her in. She felt consumed by them, unable to look away. They were smoke and fire beneath his dark lashes. She trembled at their promise. "That's good, Nikki. You were right. When I go after something I want, I don't give up until I get it. And I want you."

It wasn't poise which kept Nikki sitting perfectly still, her eyes meeting his levelly. Wine and fatigue and his hypnotic gaze had dulled her reflexes. When what he'd said sunk in, her breath caught. It was several seconds before it returned. Then, before she could think of the words to tell him off properly, Archer had lifted his glass in a mocking salute, and returned to the figures he'd been compiling.

Nikki closed her eyes and rested her head on the high back of the chair, wondering if he could have really said what she thought she'd heard. She'd think about it later. Just now, with her mind all soft and fuzzy from the wine, it was incomprehensible.

Julian sat back after a moment and contemplated the lovely woman dozing in the chair nearby. He had meant what he said. There was no question in his mind now that she was guileless; with a personal integrity that was refreshing to find in the business world. But she was an enigma, also. She had abandoned what had to be the most important aspect of her life—her art—for the questionable rewards of work in the oilfield. And, surely, a woman as attractive, as intriguing as Nicole Duval Colomb should have been involved with someone by now. He intended to find out what other surprises waited beneath the surface. The exploration should be a very interesting journey.

Nikki felt herself being lifted. Her lids opened reluctantly and her eyes half-focused on a square, sun-bronzed jaw.

"If I'm dreaming, I really should make an effort to wake up," she murmured sleepily.

"Go back to sleep." The voice was soft gravel.

It really was a delicious sensation, Nikki decided as she rested her head against a broad shoulder. The last time that she'd been carried like this was . . . over the threshold!

That thought had the effect of cold water. Her lassitude was gone. Every nerve was vibrantly alive.

"I suppose I should ask where you're taking me?" Nikki pulled away from him slightly, as far as the curl of his strong arms would allow.

Gray eyes flashed wickedly. "To bed."

Nikki swallowed. She was certain that he must feel her heart thumping against her ribs where their torsos made contact. She could certainly feel the heat pass through her from that point.

"I'm sorry," Nikki managed with some aplomb. "When you said that you wanted to go to dinner, I didn't know that I was to be the main course."

His eyes moved over her with wolfish gleam. "My dear, that's an excellent idea!" He swung her through the door of her bedroom. Nikki struggled, but with a deep chuckle Archer merely curled her more tightly against his hard-muscled chest. "I've never had a woman fight to save her virtue before," he said. "This night might prove interesting."

"Beast!"

Archer eyed the bed speculatively, testing her weight in his arms. Guessing his intent, Nikki struggled harder. "Oh, no! *Don't you dare!* Don't—O-o-o-h!"

The last ended in a strangled gasp of fury as Archer tossed her high into the air. Nikki landed in the center of the white eyelet coverlet, the French-blue silk of her skirt twisting high around her waist, exposing her pink teddy.

Archer threw back his head, laughter rumbling from his deep chest as Nikki snatched frantically at her skirt. Then, as a bedboard on the antique four-poster suddenly gave way, her feet went higher than her head. Nikki cursed impressively as she tried to tame her swirling skirt and sit up against an impossible forty-five degree angle.

"Your language is deplorable," Archer scolded at length. He was no longer laughing, but his gray eyes still danced. "Here," he commanded. "Take my hand."

Nikki seized the hand he offered and hauled herself upward as Archer leaned over to help. She saw his expression of surprise as he was pulled hopelessly off balance just before his nose met her forehead some-where in middle space. As he crashed down across her, the remaining bedboard gave way with a loud thump!

"*My* language!" Nikki snorted as his deep baritone rang out. "And get off—I'm being crushed!"

"Crushed!" Archer choked. "My nose is broken!"

"It is not," Nikki puffed, still helplessly flattened into the feather mattress by his weight. She pushed at him until he shifted his weight to the side, then drew in a deep breath.

"It *is* broken. It's bleeding."

"Bleeding? Not on my white eyelet, it's not!" Nikki gasped. Scrambling to her knees, she unceremoniously rolled him onto his back. She snatched tissues from the box on the bedside table and applied them. The damage appeared to be minor. The bleeding quickly stopped.

Archer put his hands behind his head and looked up at her. In the subdued light of the bedside lamp, the planes and angles of his face showed in sharp relief. His teeth flashed white as he smiled.

Her every cell was suddenly completely alive to him; how his greater weight sank into the mattress, compel-ling her forward, the heat of his body, the light citrus fragrance of his cologne mixing with his own male scent.

"I haven't had such simple fun in a long time," he told her. Nikki saw the look in his eyes, and she looked away.

"You mean it's been a long time since you behaved so childishly," she said. She cleared her throat lightly. Her voice sounded unnaturally husky.

"Not childishly. Childlike," he corrected her softly.

"What's wrong with that? Somehow, I get the feeling that it's been a long time since you let loose, too?" It was a question.

Sitting back on her heels, Nikki shrugged and fidgeted with the material of her skirt, all too aware of his warm gaze.

"Let me see your bump," he commanded softly. The soft rasp of his voice caressed her. Archer propped on one elbow and his long fingers brushed beneath her bangs. Nikki flinched, but not from pain.

Her freshly shampooed hair was alive with cinnamon highlights and smelled of jasmine. Archer's fingers slipped away from her forehead and splayed into its thickness, testing its weight.

"Why are you afraid?"

His question caught her off guard. All the more so because she'd just been looking for the best way to slip out of this situation before it became any more intimate than it was.

"I'm not afraid!" Nikki blurted.

"Yes, you are. And you're a remarkably bad liar, easy to see through."

His long fingers, still entangled in her hair, began to massage the sensitive hollow at the base of her skull. Ripples of sensation radiated outward from the point of contact, up over her scalp, down her spine, across her shoulder blades. How did he know just where to touch? The soft massaging action stilled her, made her want to close her eyes like a sleepy cat and just experience the sensations.

"I think you may be pretty good at lying to yourself," Archer continued. His voice had dropped to the lower registers. It caressed her softly. "If I asked you if you wanted to kiss me again you'd probably say no . . ."

"Yes! I mean, no—oh . . ." As his lips curved into a smile of victory, Nikki realized that she'd stepped into a verbal trap. He'd intended to take either answer as affirmative.

The mocking smile slowly vanished from his face. She felt little quivers of sensation trickle through her as his intention began to show in his eyes. A tiny voice warned her of the danger of becoming too physical with this handsome, too-charming man, but her limbs were leaden. The darkening look in his gray eyes was a magnet she couldn't resist.

Julian's gaze moved over her face. He felt a deep curiosity about this woman. She certainly had the power to excite him; when she looked at him like that, he felt the effect clear to his toes. But there was an enchanting vulnerability about this enigmatic brunette. Her skin was exquisitely soft to the touch as he slowly moved his thumbs down the line of her jaw until they rested lightly under her chin. With a light pressure, he pulled her toward him. There was no resistance to his pull. Nikki's eyes became languorous, the lids dropping halfway over the odd violet irises. A pulse beat throbbed in her throat.

She could feel the fan of his breath on her sensitized lips, smell the faint aromas of bourbon and cigar. Her lips, softened in anticipation, seemed to swell and yearn toward his.

Julian brushed a downy kiss on her pliant mouth, aware of an almost electric shock at the contact. He drew back, took a small breath, and pulled her lips more firmly against his as he deepened the kiss. His lips became mobile, and, with a sigh, she sank down full-length against him. He burned at the feel of her feminine curves pressing into his side. She seemed to mold into his hardness. Julian felt a jolt of desire that surprised him with its intensity. With a low moan, he dragged her lax frame on top of him. His tongue pried her lips apart and he deepened the kiss until he was searching every crevice of her mouth, tasting her tongue, her palate, the spaces between her lips and teeth. His hands traveled with a life of their own over her silk-clad back, to her softly rounded bottom. He groaned ardently at the tantalizing pressure of her belly and groin against his manhood. With gentle fingers, he drew her tighter to his hips. Little bursts of sound from her throat provoked him to rock his arousal against the mound at the juncture of her thighs.

Nikki's body seethed with need. The fervor of Julian's kiss, and the feel of his exploring hands and virile body had her gasping from wanting him. This was what she should have felt with Bob, she realized. But she hadn't. She hadn't thought that she was capable! The sensations were so new—too new. When he ground his hips against hers, she wanted to cry out from the force of her need.

Julian grasped Nikki's upper arms and effortlessly lifted her from him. The constricting clothes had to be removed. He had to feel her satin skin, touch her secret places. He sat up in the bed looking down at her trembling form beside him. Her eyes glistened as though they held unshed tears. He murmured soothing sounds as his hand undid the buttons of her dress, grazing her skin in tantalizing caresses. Her breasts, covered by a shell-pink teddy, rose and fell with each rapid breath, the nipples hardening as his fingers brushed the soft mounds.

He couldn't get enough of her, and this had just begun. His body vibrated with a tenderness and depth of feeling that shook him. He longed to give her pleasure, and to take pleasure from her.

Only then did he realize that she hadn't moved. She had never reached out to touch him, had not initiated one kiss. He searched her face in confusion, even while his hands continued uncovering her. There was no fear in her gaze. Only a kind of wonder. A second later she closed her eyes tightly, arching her body to his hands as they smoothed over her bared shoulders, her swelling breasts.

But her hands stayed at her side, fingers clenching and unclenching spasmodically.

Perhaps she was just too shy with him—a new lover. He knew so little about her. He remembered the encounter between Nikki and that gang-pusher on the tank battery. The man had accused her of pining for a dead man. Could it be that he was the first man in her life since her husband's death? His eyes scanned her face, her straining body. Was he the first in five years?

The thought sobered him. The flush on his skin cooled a little. He withdrew his hands.

Nikki lay unmoving. She waited for the delicious sensations to return, for Julian to begin again the fiery touches that her body ached for. When they didn't come, she opened her eyes. He sat beside her on the bed. His gray eyes were dark, probing. A slight frown deepened the line between his straight brows. Had she put him off in some way? She couldn't bear this waiting, not knowing. He had obviously been enjoying what he had been doing—she had felt that when she lay on top of him. What could have made him stop?

Julian looked into Nikki's wide eyes. Her expression questioned him—almost begging him. She *did* want him.

Julian's mouth curved in a gentle smile. He reached out to touch her flushed cheek. With lazy eyes and soft fingers, he traced the line of her cheek, the curve of her dark brows, the length of her imperfect nose. He was rewarded by a tiny smile that reached all the way to her eyes. It pleased him unaccountably to make her smile like that. When he sketched her lips with his finger her mouth opened and little puffs of breath tickled the stray hairs on the back of his hand. Need surged within him.

How could this girl-woman affect him so strongly with such a small action? Many more-glamorous women had left him cold. He shook his head and smiled wryly. It didn't matter. Not right now.

When he lowered his head to trail kisses from her teddy upward along her throat to the small pink earlobe revealed by her straight mahogany hair, she pushed her head back into the softness of the pillow, raising her chin and baring her throat to his lips. At the same time, he moved his hands to the thin straps of her teddy, sliding them down her arms until her breasts were free. "Beautiful," he murmured. His lips wandered sensuously back down her throat, seeking out the pink-tipped mounds. Julian nibbled at her sweetness, bathing each teasing nip with his tongue. When he pulled back to look at her, there were tiny red blushes against the pale skin where he had taken each love-bite.

Nikki was lost in a world of sensation. Each touch pulled her deeper into the vortex of flame that first flared at every point of contact, and then centered in a pulsing area of heat deep in her body.

Julian lowered his mouth to the tight pink buds that thrust upward. He sent his tongue on little teasing forays over the smooth surrounding skin, in a circle over the light pink areola, to flutter at the hard peaks. Nikki writhed beneath him, thrusting her torso involuntarily toward his torturing mouth. He held her to the bed with hands clamped gently around her upper arms. When he began to suckle tenderly, grazing the turgid nipple with his teeth, he heard a high-pitched keening begin deep in her chest. His own body swelled in response to her fervor.

Julian rolled onto the bed. Thrusting an arm beneath her throbbing body, he pulled her against him, full-length. As they lay on their sides facing each other, Julian ran his hand along her leg and under her skirt, stroking the stocking-clad softness up to the exposed bare skin between the teddy and the tops of the hose. The press of her firm breasts mashed against his chest made him want the feel of them against his bare torso.

But Nikki's hands were poised at his waist. She seemed lost in the pleasure of his busy hands—almost unaware that he was even there. He wanted her to touch him. He wanted her to be eager to feel him naked.

Julian grasped Nikki's hand and lay it against the hair curling from the opening of his shirt. Her eyes opened slightly, her gaze clearing. "Undress me." The words were meant to be a request, but the urgency he felt made them a demand.

She looked up at him, her eyes wide with shyness—and something more. As he tried to read the sudden darkness in them, her hand fell away from him. Her hesitation filled him with frustration. He was so aroused. He wanted this woman with a strange inner intensity, but her shyness puzzled him. How could she just lay there when it was obvious that what she felt was just as strong?

Julian touched her troubled face. He smoothed the little creases gently from her forehead. "You're so beautiful, Nikki. I want to bring you pleasure. But I don't understand. Am I moving too fast for you?"

The dark look in her eyes cleared a little. She wet

her lips with the tip of her tongue. She made a small negative gesture with her head and her lids lowered.

"Then please, Nikki, touch me." He pulled her tighter to him, making her feel how aroused he was.

Her face was a mask. He could feel her muscles growing tense.

"Nikki, I don't want to make love *to* you! I want to make love *with* you. Slowly. Over and over again." His voice seductive.

"I . . . can't," she said in a harsh whisper.

"Of course, you can. You're not frigid. You want me as badly as I want you."

All she heard was that word. Frigid. The word Bob had always used so hurtfully. Making her a failure— again. The rushing pleasure drained from her, leaving a kind of dead emptiness behind. She pushed against Julian's chest, but he held tighter.

"Damn it, Nikki! What's the matter? I want to know what's wrong."

"I thought you said I was transparent."

Her retreat from him didn't make sense. "I said you couldn't lie for beans." With his free hand, he raised her face, forcing her to look at him. "I felt the response in you. You're not cold. Why won't you touch me?" He saw pain flash in her eyes.

With a look of shock, she twisted out of his grasp. She was off the bed and adjusting her clothing before he could restrain her.

"Why don't you tell me what you want from me? You're the expert here."

"Expert?" He felt suddenly cold inside.

"You know. Playing games is a specialty with you, isn't it?"

He was taken aback. His face grew dark and forbidding. "Just what the hell do you mean by that?"

"I shouldn't have to spell it out for you." She stood before him, trembling with rage, hugging her arms to herself. Shutting him out. "If you'd just tell me what you want, we could get this over with." Her tone was scathing. "You're the boss. Tell me how far I have to go to save our contract, and I'll decide if the kickback is too high."

"Are you accusing me of bargaining for sexual favors?"

"If that's what it takes."

Her quavering voice infuriated him even more. Nikki cowered from the dark intent in his eyes.

Julian caught her and tumbled her back onto the broken bed. "If that's what it takes, you're willing, huh?" he asked darkly. His sudden brutal kiss ground her lips against her teeth. The violence of it demanded that she fight back. Her fear of him held her immobile.

Julian continued the savage kiss until he realized that Nikki wasn't moving—wasn't struggling to free herself as he'd expected, putting the lie to her words. He drew back, and looked down into a face pale and taut with fear. He felt a shudder run through her.

A wave of self-disgust doused his anger. He cursed himself silently. It didn't matter if she'd goaded him, he'd had no right to do this to her.

Julian thrust himself up off the bed. Nikki lay as he had left her, her clothes disheveled, her hair spread like a fan behind her head; her lip quivered and her eyes tightly closed.

Julian stared at her, then shook his head.

When Nikki opened her eyes again, the door had closed behind him.

FOUR

The next afternoon, Nikki knocked loudly on Mrs. DesHotel's door. While she waited, she admired the garden. Jonquils and tulips nodded in the spring sunshine and pansies made bright patches of velvety color in the window boxes. Bees moved lazily between the blossoms, adding their pleasant drone to the calls of a pair of mockingbirds high in the moss-draped oaks.

Nikki knocked again. The old lady was a bit deaf. After a moment she heard footsteps, and a high-pitched voice called out. "I'm coming. I'm coming." And then, "No, Mignon, you can't go out right now."

"Hello, Nikki," Mrs. DesHotels said in her faintly-accented English when she opened the door. "*Quoi ca dit?*" she added in French. Her lively pale-blue eyes twinkled behind her bifocals as though she had some secret to share.

"*Pas rien,*" Nikki answered. Nothing, indeed.

"Come in, come in. Have some coffee with me. I just made a fresh pot."

"No, thank you. I just wanted to borrow a hammer, if you have one. My bed broke." The gleam in Mrs.

DesHotel's eyes brightened and her ever-present smile grew even larger.

"Ah, *cher*, you don't need that hammer." She reached out and drew Nikki into the house.

"I beg your pardon . . . ?" Nikki wondered if she'd been misunderstood.

"That nice young man already fixed the bed." Mrs. DesHotels positively gleamed.

"Nice young man . . . ?" Nikki had a sinking feeling.

"Why, yes. He said he broke it, so he came to fix it. I let him in myself, while you were out." Nikki's cheeks flamed. "We had coffee," Mrs. DesHotels continued. "And a nice long talk." She draped a companionable arm around Nikki's waist and pulled her into the kitchen.

And Mrs. DesHotels could really talk, Nikki thought. She was mortified as she imagined just what the old lady had had to say.

The tiny woman had gone out of her way to befriend Nikki. She had also shown a singleminded determination to see Nikki properly married again. Oh, yes, she could imagine what the landlady had said.

Damn Julian Archer! What was he doing back here again?

Mrs. DesHotels put a brimming coffee cup on the table in front of her. Nikki sipped distractedly, her mind in turmoil. When the older woman sat down in the chair across the table, she looked up absently.

"So handsome," Mrs. DesHotel's tossed out like a lure. Nikki ignored it. "So tall. So well-mannered." And so exasperating, Nikki thought.

"Mmmm . . ." Nikki murmured noncommittally. If he'd undergone one of Mrs. D's examinations, Nikki was sure her landlady would know as much about Julian Archer as she did.

Later, as she opened the door to her apartment, her eyes moved with some trepidation around the room. She found the sweet scent before her gaze came to rest on the flowers. Arranged in her favorite Tiffany glass vase were at least a dozen yellow roses. A small white card hung conspicuously from a piece of the surrounding greenery.

"You still owe me a night out," he had written on the note. "I'll pick you up Wednesday night at seven-thirty. Wear something silk again."

"Well, of all the arrogant . . . !" she sputtered. She was still terribly embarrassed over last night's fiasco. Truthfully, she couldn't understand why he wanted to see her again.

She'd had a feeling the first time she met him that this man was going to complicate her life. Now she was sure of it.

"It sure is a hot one!" Nikki lifted her thick hair and wiped her neck with a crumpled red bandana. She walked across the cluttered office to the window air conditioner. She stood before it with her hand behind her head, letting the air cool her sweaty neck. "Gina, has Pop come in yet this morning?"

Gina Meaux, the part-time secretary who handled the minor office work and bookkeeping for Colomb Contractors, was typing a barge run. The clatter of the typewriter keys continued for a few seconds. Then the woman turned to face Nikki. "I've been meaning to talk to you about that, Nikki. Pop is here less and less these days. Joseph Bascomb from Turner Production called three times today to talk to him. You know I can only help the clients on small things. I can't keep putting him off forever."

"I know, Gina." Nikki sighed wearily. "I've tried talking to Pop about it, but he just won't let me find someone to take over for me in the field. And he keeps so much of the client dealings to himself. It's like pulling teeth to get him to let me help." Nikki found herself wishing that Bob was still alive. Pop wouldn't have hesitated to turn things over to his son, but sometimes he acted like he didn't trust Nikki to do things correctly.

"Look," Gina said, "the rumors about this business with Archer have gotten around. A lot of the clients are calling to find out about our involvement. They've heard Archer is gonna dump us. Is it true, Nikki?"

What could Nikki tell her? That Archer Oil *had* been about to dump Colomb until she'd worked it out with Julian Archer? An image of his face filled her mind and she angrily banished it. "We'll still be operating their lease. I don't think the company is in any danger of losing the contract."

Not if he'd meant what he said about the painting, she thought. Her instincts told her that Julian Archer was a man of integrity. That's why he expected it— demanded it—in others. She respected that in him, as a man of business. On a personal level, she didn't want anything more to do with him.

"Pop acted like he didn't know anything was going on when I asked him about it yesterday. But I could tell something was worrying him. And he got really upset when I told him you had taken the Archer records home last week to go over them. He ranted and raved so loud I thought he was gonna have another attack." Gina looked at Nikki with a sheepish expression. "He told me that those records are private, and that you had no right to go into them. I hope I didn't mess things up for you by telling him.''

"It's okay, Gina. I'll talk to him about it.'' Nikki moved to the door of the second office. "I have a few things to discuss with him myself,'' she mumbled to herself.

Half-an-hour later, as Nikki sat trying to concentrate on some paperwork at the small desk in the corner of the office, her phone buzzed. "Yes, Gina.''

"Nikki!'' The secretary sounded agitated. "There's a call for you on one. It's Julian Archer!''

"What is this? ESP?'' Nikki grumbled. But she couldn't deny a sudden leaping excitement.

"Nicole Duval Colomb, *you* are an idiot,'' Nikki told her reflection as she removed the last hot roller from her hair. "You don't even like the man—why are you letting him maneuver you into going out with him? Again?'' Well, she didn't have a choice, did she? She'd agreed to one date, and he was going to hold her to it. She bent over, vigorously brushing her hair upside down, then tossed it back into place as she straightened. Her wedge cut swung with added fullness. She pulled one side back with a sparkling comb and surveyed the results.

Anticipation fluttered like so many butterflies in her stomach. No, Nikki decided, she definitely didn't *like* Julian Archer. One moment, she felt an active dislike; the next, she felt weak in the knees. He was far too exciting for *like*. And completely exasperating.

She was appalled with herself for being this excited at the prospect of dinner with him—especially after the debacle of the other evening! But she *was* excited by the prospect. Their last encounter had ended in disaster, but she couldn't forget he'd shown her that she could feel. Little waves of remembered passion trickled through her and she shivered.

When Nikki answered the doorbell a few minutes later, she was glad she'd followed the hint on the card, which had come with the roses, and had dressed with care. Her dress, an ice-blue silk-and-wool blend that was suitable for the cool spring evening, had dramatic dolman sleeves and a deep neckline. It was held together by a wide belt that flattered her trim waist. The skirt hugged her hips as she walked.

"Hello." Julian was elegant in a dark dinner jacket. The light spice of his cologne caused Nikki to draw a deep breath as he stepped past her into the apartment.

Julian held a bearded iris out to her and smiled as she took it. He'd been right. The fragile bloom was the same shade as her blue-violet eyes. His gaze swept over her appreciatively. "Are you ready?"

Although his tone seemed straightforward enough, she examined the question for double meaning. Finding none, she nodded. "I'll get my purse."

"Better bring a light coat. It may get cool," he called after her, making her wonder what he had in mind.

As Julian settled her into the car, he wasn't surprised to see the curtain of Mrs. DesHotel's kitchen window drop back into place. He smiled to himself. The morning he'd fixed the bed, that charming old lady had craftily pumped him for information, all the while painting an image that made Nikki a paragon. There should be a sign on the landlady's door reading: DANGER: MATCHMAKER WITHIN, he thought as he slipped behind the wheel.

"Now, may I ask where we're going?" Nikki asked.

"As I told you on the phone, it's a surprise," he replied with a smile that infuriated her.

Julian backed the luxury sedan onto the street and shifted into drive. The slight smile still curved one corner of his mouth as he allowed Nikki to lapse into a stiff silence that spoke eloquently of how she felt about being in his company.

But a reflective frown soon deepened the slight line between his dark brows as he considered the errors in judgment he had made about this woman. She had caught his interest from the moment she had stormed Grimes's office. His greatest mistake had been to assume that, once he'd pulled back a few layers, she would prove to be like most of the other women he had known. But he had found that the layers didn't peel back quite so readily. The small peek he'd had beneath the surface had shown Nikki to be unique.

She was like the painting he'd taken. It was a small canvas which had been displayed apart from the main grouping. It had been the first thing which caught his eye as he'd walked into her parlor the other evening. It had appeared at first glance to be a simple hunting scene. But it had drawn his eye back; compelled him to look deeper.

"Nicole, I won't try to make excuses for my behavior the other night. I was an ass. But you were damn provoking. You're very good at provoking me, in a number of ways."

"And you're very good at being an ass."

Julian glanced at her sharply. "I said I'm sorry."

"No," she corrected him. "You said that you were an ass. I agreed. I can't believe that you've manipulated me into going out with you again!"

"I didn't exactly manipulate you. I caught you on a technicality. You promised to have dinner with me and you never did." Humor sparked in his eyes. "Besides, you'd be the first to tell me that you wouldn't be here if I'd left you any options. Then I'd never have had the chance to make it up to you for being an ass.''

"And that's *not* manipulation?" said Nikki. "All right. I'll play by your rules—so long as *you* play by them, too. You've never admitted that your accusations about Colomb were wrong, but it doesn't matter. You have the painting you took the other night. As I remember the offer you made, that squares our account. After tonight, we're quits."

Archer drove in silence for a few moments, then pulled into a parking lot near the river. They hadn't driven far. For an instant a thoughtful look claimed his face, then it was gone. He smiled. "You don't dust very often, do you?"

"I beg your par—" Nikki began, but the man was already out of the car and moving around to her side.

"You're right. We have been playing by my rules," Julian said as he helped her out. "So now, it's only fair to reverse that."

"What do you mean?" she asked suspiciously.

"Simple. Whatever happens between us—" his smoky gaze moved over her face and snagged her mouth, reminding her vividly of everything that *had* happened between them, "—is your choice."

"Whatever happens?" She swallowed, wondering why her voice came out so throaty.

"Whatever happens. I'm ready, willing, and available. But from this moment forward, I refuse to initiate so much as a handshake. You write the script . . . unless you're afraid?"

"Of what?"

"That you'll find out you're here not because I forced you, but because you want to be."

Nikki's mouth opened. No words came out. Before she could find words strong enough to tell him how preposterous such an idea was, Julian was guiding her forward.

"I hope you're hungry. Come on, it's almost time to sail."

"Sail?"

"Sail."

For the first time, she realized that their destination was the replica of an old-time river steamboat at the dock, and not the nearby restaurant. Strings of fairy lights outlined the boat against the night-dark Vermilion. Light spilled from the grand salon. A maitre'd was waiting to show them to their table on the fantail under the stars.

"The whole boat, Julian?" Nikki asked him later. She'd had an excellent dinner of blackened redfish, crawfish bisque, and steamed vegetables—all served with the sauce of Archer's compelling charm. It would have been impossible not to enjoy the meal.

"It seemed the thing to do. This was the only evening that I could get away this week. The *Vermilion Queen* doesn't normally run on Wednesdays, which suited me just fine. I didn't want to share you with a bunch of tourists."

"So you chartered the boat and arranged for catering. You've spent a mint on charters lately. Trying to impress me with your fortune?"

Julian's mustache spread in a smile as the night wind ruffled his dark hair. "Why? Would it work?"

Nikki returned his smile. One day he would probably put the name Duval together with New Orleans and come up with banking. No, money had never been a problem in her life; therefore it didn't impress her. She certainly didn't equate it with happiness. She thought of the money her father still sent every month, even though she was twenty-six. A balm for his conscience,

she supposed, since she hadn't seen him since she was
five. Money could satisfy only material needs, not those
even more basic than food and shelter. The funds went
coldly and impersonally into her checking account by
direct deposit. He didn't even have to sign a check.

No, she wasn't impressed by Archer's money. She
was impressed by the business genius which had
allowed him to amass it. She didn't even believe that
money was important to him. Challenge for that keen
intelligence was what he would thrive on. Money, she
thought wryly, was probably just a convenient way to
keep score.

Nikki pushed away the dessert of fresh pears with
lemon sauce she'd been toying with and touched her
napkin to her lips. Beyond the railing, an almost-full
moon was rising above the cypress trees along the riv-
erbank. In their wake, it spread a silvery carpet edged
with frothy lace spun by the side wheels. Music from
the string quartet in the salon floated out to them, and
Nikki hummed along with the popular romantic ballad.

"Nice music," she murmured. She hadn't danced
for a long, long time. She wanted very much to dance,
now, with this tall man.

"Mmmm. Very." Julian agreed, his eyes twinkling.
Nikki looked at him expectantly. It was a few moments
before she realized that he wasn't going to ask her. He
was waiting for her to ask him. *You write the script*,
he'd said.

"Would you care to dance?" she laughed.

"I thought you'd never ask." He grinned, a flash of
white teeth in the half-light.

As his hand at the small of her back pulled her close,
Nikki closed her eyes and gave herself up to the music
and his touch.

They danced for a time, not speaking. The tempo of

the music picked up. Nikki found herself pressed even closer to Julian's long form as she followed him in more intricate dance steps. Then, when the musicians paused at the end of the song, he didn't immediately relinquish his hold on her. She looked up into his shadowed face, a little breathless from exertion. And something more.

"They have to break sometime," Julian said regretfully.

"Yes. I guess so," Nikki agreed. He held her close a moment longer, as if he was reluctant to let her go.

Nikki looked out over the water and toyed with one of his shirt studs. She enjoyed the luxury of being held against his firm chest. "The river is really beautiful by night," she said. "By day it's too filled with silt, too muddy. Horrible tasting, too—I almost drowned in it once."

Julian's hand tightened around her waist. "Maybe this wasn't a good idea."

"Oh, no! It's lovely," she assured him. "I'm not even sure why I told you that. It happened a long time ago and a long way downriver from here. Besides, the Vermilion coils like a snake through the parish and splits Abbeville into halves. There's no way to avoid it. I cross it so many times a day I seldom think about it anymore." Liar, she told herself. But she felt foolish for having mentioned it. She wasn't going to bore him with her occasional bad dream.

Julian pressed a warm kiss on the top of her head. "That's for not drowning."

"You're welcome," Nikki told him quietly.

"Would you like some cognac?" he asked, relaxing his hold.

"No. But coffee would be nice."

He reseated her at the table and instructed the waiter,

who'd appeared as if by telepathy. Julian soon had her laughing at several misadventures from what must have been a precocious childhood. Nikki offered a few tidbits from her own, but Julian arched a skeptical brow when she avowed that she almost never got into a scrape.

"I can hardly remember scuffing my Mary-Janes," Nikki laughed.

"So how did a nice girl like you end up in a hard hat in the oilfield?"

Nikki's eyes dropped to her coffee cup. "Archer Oil's safety regulations require one, I think," she quiped lightly.

"Nikki, why do you do that?"

"What?"

"Every time we talk about anything more personal than the weather, your shields go up."

"I . . . I guess I'm just a private person. I don't know you that well." A blush stole up her neck and into her cheeks as she remembered how intimately they had *almost* known each other. From the glint in his eyes, she guessed that Julian was thinking the same thing. His gaze dropped to her mouth, and from there to the shadowy cleft at the vee of her neckline, and her blush deepened.

"I'm trying to rectify that." He lifted her hand and examined the long supple fingers with their short, well-groomed nails—so much more attractive than fashionable inch-long claws. And, such gifted hands, he thought.

"My husband lost interest in college after an injury ended his football career." She couldn't prevent herself from pulling her hand away. She lifted her coffee cup as if that had been her purpose, and held it in both hands. "After he'd recovered, he went to work for the company. This was at about the same time my father-in-law's doctor warned him to slow down, so it worked out well. Or it would have. Bob died in that stupid accident . . .'' Nikki cleared her throat and sipped her coffee, hoping to gain control over her voice; aware that Archer might misinterpret the cause. ''Bob was Pop's pride. His eldest son. I think the shock of it caused Pop's first heart attack. I pitched-in to fill the gap while he recuperated. Then he had a second attack. After that, I guess—like you—I just inherited the job.''

''Is that when you *quit* painting? When your husband died?''

He watched as she folded her hands and tucked them beneath the table. But she met his gaze squarely. ''I never quit painting. *It quit me.* For a long time after the accident, I was just too caught up in other things. Then, when I went back . . . oh, I can move paint from palette to canvas. But the result is flat, one dimensional. I might as well be painting by numbers. I can't even get excited about painting anymore. And there's no use forcing it. I've tried.''

She lifted her coffee again, but her hand shook and she set the cup down abruptly. She started to draw her hand under the table again, but Julian caught it. His thumb brushed her palm, sending an arc of electricity clear to her toes.

''You know, that's a lovely song they're playing,'' he murmured after an instant.

Nikki summoned up a smile. ''You wouldn't be trying to *initiate* something, would you?''

His eyes held a devilish glint. ''How could you think that after I gave you my word?'' He helped her out of her chair and she was soon in his arms again.

For a long time Nikki was content just to be in the circle of Julian Archer's strong arms as they danced. There, it was easy to forget the disappointments of the past and the uncertainty of a future that seemed gray and unfulfilling. It was like stepping out of time for a moment into a pleasant fantasy.

"Nikki?"

She looked up into his face, darkly handsome in the moonlight reflected from the water, his eyes almost mirror-silver. No, she thought. This was too compelling to be a fantasy. And there was no such thing as a fairy-tale ending.

"What's that wonderful scent?" he asked, trying to ignore how her hips pressed into his when she leaned back within the circle of his arms. Her heels made her nearly the same height. He was already very much aware of the sensuous softness of the fabric of her dress and the way her body heat passed through it beneath his hands.

Nikki inhaled deeply as she surveyed the dark wooded bank of the river. "Wild honeysuckle. In some places it grows quite thick." She sniffed the air again. "It is lovely."

As she'd turned her head, her neckline had pulled open further, giving him a delectable glimpse of the swell of her breasts. Julian couldn't help remembering how they had looked as he had exposed them, how exquisitely soft her skin had felt to his fingers and mouth, how it had tasted . . . Julian felt Nikki stiffen as her body correctly interpreted the warm tension building in his loins.

"Is it just me, Nikki?" he asked in sudden exasperation. "Did what happened between us the other night give you a disgust for being close to me? I never intended to go through with taking you in that way, you know. I wanted you to fight me. I wanted to prove that what you said was a lie, that you didn't believe that you had to be with me to help your company, but that you wanted to be with me." His fingers caught a strand of her hair. "Maybe that's not what came across."

Julian's face was suffused with remorse and sincerity. Nikki stared up at him, wide-eyed. "No! I . . . oh, no!"

"Then . . . ?"

"I shouldn't have said those things." Her words came out in a rush. "I was . . . confused. No. That's not the truth. I was embarrassed. I . . . it had been a long time. I've only been with Bob and . . . it . . ."

Julian turned away from her and banged the flat of his hand on the rail. Having her words confirm what he'd suspected made him surprisingly angry. "So, you quit painting when your husband died and you quit . . . everything." He drew in a deep breath and released it. He went on more softly. "He must have been quite a guy for a woman like you to stay true to his memory all this time."

Julian wasn't sure what he'd been expecting. It wasn't Nikki's laughter. Something in the sound of it set his teeth on edge. "What the hell!" His strong fingers closed over her shoulders and he dragged her backward against him. She tilted her head back against his shoulder, the bitter laughter changing to silent shaking paroxysms. "What the hell's so—"

"Funny?" Nikki gasped. "Oh, everything. Everything." Her voice was stinging. "Let me try again. My marriage was . . . *not* a success."

The courtship, now, she thought, that had been a thing of beauty. Bob had made her feel completely necessary to his life. It had been such a novel feeling, to be important to someone. It had been the answer to a secret dream she had hardly even admitted to herself. And if she had picked up warning signals of trouble ahead in the last couple of weeks before the ceremony, then she had put it down to ordinary cold feet. Bob had needed her.

His need had soon stifled her. Smothered her.

Nikki turned and looked up into Julian's dark face. His features were still, expressionless, but his eyes were warm as he waited for whatever she would tell him. "In no way was it a success," she went on harshly, her arms crossed over her chest. "It was so much not a success that I never cared to have another relationship. When Bob and I were dating, I wanted . . . but after we were married I thought that I was one of those women who just can't feel anything. I never *did*."

Then you came along and suddenly I'm swamped by all these sensations I don't know how to handle, she thought to herself. *I feel . . . like I'm sliding up a rainbow. I feel these little rockets going off inside. I'm twenty-six years old and for the first time I feel like a woman! Almost a complete woman.*

"When you asked me to . . . touch you, to actively give back to you what you were giving me, I froze. I wanted to move . . . but I just couldn't. I felt so . . . gauche and immature, and I acted gauche and immature. I'm surprised I didn't make you disgusted with me."

Julian's hands had slipped up her arms to her shoulders and were gently massaging away the tension he'd found there. He looked down into her wide, vulnerable eyes and smiled. "Nikki, whether you realize it or not, you're a very sensual woman. You have a great deal of passion within you. Circumstances, or whatever, may have caused you to tuck it away, leave it untapped. But you'll have it when you're ready."

Julian leaned back against the high railing, and Nikki found herself fitted between his long legs. He brushed her bangs away from her forehead, sending delicious little shivers along her nerve endings at the contact. "You interest me greatly—in that male-female way. You're much too attractive not to. But I'm past the age when I find a purely sexual relationship satisfying. You interest me, Nikki, on a great many levels.

"The past is gone. We have no control over that. But the future . . . remember, Nikki, whatever develops between us is completely up to you," Julian rasped softly. "For instance, if you wanted to kiss me right now, *you'd* have to do it."

She rose up on her toes with the help of his steadying hands at her waist and shyly brushed her lips over his.

"That's my girl," Julian murmured, folding her closer. Then his mouth claimed hers in return, in a kiss which sent a current of desire down into the most secret part of her. The intensity of his kiss deepened and his lips grew more demanding as they moved over hers. Nikki quickly lost all sense of time and place. She delighted in the feel of his heart thumping rapidly in his chest where her breast pressed against it, and she unconsciously tightened her hold. As Julian's tongue reacquainted itself with all the secret places of her mouth, the warm need he'd caused to erupt within her began to grow, to swell.

Julian sensed her body's demand for greater intimacies. His own responded. But he gave her no more than she actively requested. He held her to him, palms cupping the back of her head, fingers splayed into her hair. He longed to mold her to him and to press her against his arousal, to show her what she had the power to do to him. He longed to expose her breasts. He imagined how beautiful they would be in the moonlight.

With a low moan, Julian pulled his lips from hers. Nikki found herself looking up into smoky slits in a face dark with desire. Without a word, he folded her to him and rested his forehead against hers. His every muscle seemed rigid, tense. She listened to the harsh rasp of his breathing become more normal, along with her own. But she was still too unsure to test the limits of his control. Could he really have meant what he'd said?

Later, Julian unlocked the door to her apartment and placed Nikki's keys in her hand. He cupped her face in his warm hands and kissed her forehead lightly.

"I enjoyed this evening very much," she admitted shyly.

The corners of his mouth twitched up in a smile, but his lids drooped, hiding the expression in his eyes. "I'm glad," he told her. "So did I."

Nikki gathered her courage. "Could you get away this coming Friday—maybe in the afternoon?" she asked hopefully.

Julian's smile deepened. "I don't know. I haven't thought of any way to force you into my loathsome company yet. Maybe if I work on it hard . . ."

Nikki's eyes dropped to the toe of her shoe. "It's not loathsome," she said quietly.

"I still don't know . . . you don't have designs on my body do you?"

"Well, if you don't want to just say—"

"I want," Julian cut her off.

"Good." Nikki dared to look up and meet his eyes. "Let me know where to pick you up. And dress casually."

Dark brows rose with interest. "Where are you spiriting me away to?"

Nikki smiled enigmatically. "That's a surprise."

As soon as Nikki drove into the parking area at the Crawfish Festival fairgrounds, Julian could hear the music. People were everywhere, and some of them were dancing to the throbbing beat as they walked. In the distance, he could see the outline of carnival rides against the sky, but all the people seemed to be heading toward the music.

"Well, shall we join them?" Nikki asked as she swung out of the driver's seat. Julian followed her, enjoying the view as they walked. She had worn a pair of faded blue jeans that clung to her hips like a hug. A bright aqua man's shirt was tied at her waist over a snug fitting tank top. The whole effect, accented by her hair pulled back in combs on each side of her head, made her look like a teenager.

Now she glanced back over her shoulder at him, the grin widening again. "C'mon, slow poke! We'll miss Rockin' Doopsie."

By the time Julian caught up to her, they had emerged from between two wooden booths into a large open area. To their right was a stage hung with bunting where long tables had been set up. A huge circle of open booths surrounded the grassy area and disappeared into the distance. Colorful flags flew everywhere, and people milled about, going from booth to booth. There was a sea of mud in the open space, but none of the fairgoers seemed to care. Most were sloshing barefoot across the space.

To the left was a flatbed semi-trailer. Sound equipment had been set up on this makeshift stage, and people were crowded about twenty deep in front. The music that blasted over the area was raucous, with a heavy rock beat, but with a completely unique flavor.

The band was composed of black men. The lead singer was an older man, and the words he was singing were French, Julian was sure, but even more heavily accented than Cajun.

Grasping his hand, Nikki pulled him through the crowd. Immediately in front of the bandstand several couples were doing what resembled an enthusiastic jitterbug.

"By the way," she asked with a sudden frown, "you do *like* crawfish, don't you?"

He glanced about him at the exuberant faces in the crowd. Some of the people held paper plates filled with the "mudbugs." "If I didn't, I'd never admit it here," he told her.

Nikki leaned back against Julian's chest and he wrapped his arms around her as the almost primitive music beat through them. "So this is *zydeco*?" he asked. It was like nothing he'd ever heard before. There were elements of jazz and also of the local French-Acadian music, but played to a strident rock beat.

The leader of the band was dressed in a conservative suit. The other band members wore everything from jeans and T-shirts to orange satin. The musician in orange satin wore sunglasses and a tall black hat that seemed to be a part of him. He wore a corrugated piece of metal, like a washboard, across his chest. He scrubbed at the instrument with thumb-picks while he danced all around the stage. The band leader played an accordion to the throbbing beat of the electric bass and drums.

Nikki noticed Julian swaying and tapping his boot to the beat. "It's infectious, isn't it?" she said loudly. He nodded, his eyes on the dancers.

"You want to try?"

His expression was dubious, but he was saved from having to answer when the music stopped and the band began to put their instruments away. The people near them began to drift toward the stage as an announcement came over the loudspeaker that the crawfish-eating contest would be starting in ten minutes.

"Crawfish eating?" he asked. "How many or how fast?" Nikki stifled a grin. He settled himself to watch, an arm around her shoulders.

"How fast," Nikki replied. "The one who can peel and eat the most boiled crawfish in fifteen minutes wins a trophy and a kiss from the festival queen." She indicated a pretty blonde of about eighteen standing on the stage.

"Exactly who enters this contest?"

"Oh, a few local politicians usually have a go at it, and occasionally some company CEO," Nikki answered. "By the way, you do know how to peel a boiled crawfish, don't you?"

He gave a vague shake of his head as he watched a couple sitting near the stage, a shallow cardboard box filled with steaming crawfish positioned between them. Nikki went over to the couple and came back carrying two crawfish in a paper towel. "Hold this," she commanded, thrusting one into his hands. He bounced the hot crawfish back and forth between his palms. "Watch closely—it's easy." She used her own to demonstrate. "You hold the crawfish in one hand and twist the tail off with the other." She pitched the head in a nearby trash barrel. "Now, crack the shell on the tail by pinching it; peel off the first two sections of the shell, and squeeze the bottom of the tail—kind of like a toothpaste tube—and the meat comes out like so. Here." She popped it into his mouth. "How's that?"

"Good," he mumbled around the delicacy. "A little spicy."

"I'm glad you like it," she said. "Now, you try."

Nikki laughed at his attempts to tear away the shell. Finally he got the tidbit out and stuffed it into her mouth. Her eyes gleamed mischievously as she chewed the mutilated piece of seafood. "Good luck," she said.

Before Julian could ask, "What for?" the voice of the announcer on stage captured his attention.

"And a last minute entry, Julian Archer of Archer Oil. That don't sound like no Cajun to me—ah, it says on the card that he's from Houston—we got us a Texan in the contest, folks!"

Julian glowered at Nikki. "You didn't! So that's what you've been grinning about." She laughed and pushed him toward the platform, to the applause of the crowd.

"You owe me one," Julian told her later as they explored the midway. Despite his inexperience, he'd acquitted himself credibly.

"Oh, no, not again!" she moaned.

"Well," he relented, "maybe only a little one."

He won a small plush panda for her at the shooting gallery. Nikki, not to be outdone, bought a crawfish stickpin and presented it to him. "You can wear it on your Stetson," she told him. They shared a cotton candy as they wandered toward the amusement rides.

"That looks interesting," Julian said, eyeing something called The Octopus.

"I don't like those," Nikki said with a shiver. She tore off part of the air-spun sugar candy and stuffed it in his mouth. Julian playfully caught her finger between his lips.

"Why?" he asked as Nikki reclaimed her hand.

"Because spinning around at ninety miles an hour, upside down and backwards, thirty-feet off the ground is not my idea of fun."

He grinned wickedly. "Yes, but you owe me one."

She paled. "Oh, please—not that one," she begged, looking up at it.

Seeing that she was truly afraid, Julian relented. He looked around to see what else was available. "How about the Ferris wheel, then?" he asked. "That should be tame enough."

Nikki swallowed convulsively as Julian dragged her toward the ticket booth. As he bought the tickets, she eyed the double Ferris wheel with trepidation. It had to be at least a thousand feet high, she decided. And all held together with those thin little cables. She felt a last minute urge to beg for a reprieve as they were ushered into the flimsy looking seat. It would never hold both of them, surely. The click of the restraining bar sliding into place was like a death knell.

"Don't look so worried—what could happen?" Julian said cheerfully.

Nikki gave him a baleful look, but refused to speculate. She closed her eyes against the sinking feeling in her stomach as the wheel started to life.

"Nikki?" She felt his arms go around her. "Relax. Nothing's going to happen."

Oh, yeah, she thought viciously, *plenty could happen. I could throw up in your lap!*

The ride seemed to go on forever. Just as she felt that she couldn't take anymore, she felt the wheel come to a halt. With a sigh of relief, she opened her eyes. "Oh, my God!" Instead of being comfortably near the ground, their seat rocked threateningly to and fro as they hung at the top of the world. Nikki flung her arms around Julian's neck, hanging on for dear life. If she hadn't been so terrified, she might have noticed his delighted expression.

"Hey, are you trying to initiate something here?" he asked her, enjoying the feel of her supple body pressed so tightly against his own.

"Oh, Julian!" Nikki cried, torn between an urge to kill him and fear of rocking their seat.

"Hey, I told you that I'm available, but *this* might be a little acrobatic."

"Julian!" Nikki laughed at the picture his words conjured up, but clasped him even tighter as the wheel jerked to a start.

Nikki's knees wobbled when she finally escaped from the ride. Julian's arm around her waist kept her steady until she got her land legs back. They walked companionably back down the midway, stopping occasionally to watch others try their luck at the games.

"What next?" Julian asked, as they ate heaping plates of crawfish etouffee served over beds of steaming rice.

"It's nearly time for the *fais-dodo,*" Nikki said. "Paul Daigle's band is playing tonight. You do like French-Acadian music, don't you?"

"I've heard it a few times," he said. "But I've never danced to it."

"Well, it's usually the waltz or the two-step," Nikki told him. "I think you can handle that."

The music cranked up as the sun left its last fading streaks of orange in the sky. The "dance floor" was larger than it had been when they'd arrived. Grandparents sat in lounge chairs around the open space and little children napped on blankets near their parents.

Julian and Nikki found a fairly dry patch of grass, and sat together in the fading light. The sound of the French accordion and the fiddle joined in a haunting wail as the first waltz began. Couples made their way to the front of the bandstand, and twirled to the strains of poignant melody.

Julian sat cross-legged on the tuft of grass, his lean leg muscles outlined by the snug jeans. When Nikki looked up at him he smiled at her, his eyes crinkling at the corners. She reached out to take his hand and was surprised that the gesture felt so natural.

They laughed together at the antics of some of the dancers when the band swung into a fast number. One of the women ended up on her behind in the mud when her partner swung her a little too hard. It didn't bother her in the least; she just got up and pushed him into the nearest puddle.

As the evening progressed, Julian found himself really enjoying the family atmosphere. A mother sat nearby, feeding her infant with a bottle. Two children, about five or six years old, danced among the legs of the adults and teens. A pair of preteen girls danced a frenzied jitterbug together. An old man of at least eighty whirled a young woman, who from the matching noses had to be a relative, around in a kind of jig. The unique music flowed around the assemblage, one minute soft and melancholy, the next loud and cheerful.

Nikki's feet had begun to fall asleep from sitting in

one position for too long. With a groan she heaved herself up and offered her hand to Julian. "You've watched for long enough," she said. "Time to face the music."

Julian grinned back at her. "I can handle a waltz, ma'am," he drawled. "But this two-step is different from what we call a two-step in Texas."

"C'mon. I can teach you." She looked down at his size twelves. "Unless those are both lefties."

After the first few turns, during which Julian watched her feet, he pulled her against him and took the lead. He caught on quickly, even adding a few flourishes of his own. "Show off," Nikki derided. "You knew how to do this all along."

"No—I've just been watching how its done. Seems that here even the littlest child knows how. I couldn't let those two show me up." He pointed to the pair of preschoolers.

The band finished the two-step, and began a plaintive waltz. Julian pulled Nikki close, his thighs hugging hers as they moved in unison with the other dancers. Her surroundings seemed to spin while she kept her eyes on his.

"What's this one called?" he asked, without relinquishing her gaze. "I can't quite make out the words."

"It's an old one, 'Un Autre Soir Ennuyant,' " she said softly. She hesitated, then translated. "Another Lonely Night.' "

"It doesn't have to be." He smiled down at her, his gaze causing a fluttering in her midsection. "There I go, initiating again," he teased. The smoky look in his eyes belied his light tone.

The waltz ended, but Julian kept her firmly in his arms. "But you initiate so well." Nikki's eyes were as dark as his.

* * *

Julian unlocked the door of the corporate apartment and swung it wide. Nikki looked in on a sea of cream colored carpet and promptly bent to unlace her muddy shoes.

"You don't have to do that," Julian's deep voice held a whisper of amusement. "There's a maid service."

"Oh, yes, I do!" Nikki informed him. "My Aunt Rosalie would spin in her grave if I walked over *that* in *these*." Julian laughed but followed her lead, leaving his boots and socks in the hallway beside her joggers.

The plush pile felt luxuriant beneath Nikki's bare feet, and she worked her toes down into it. The atmosphere of the apartment was relaxed, elegant. Mauve, yellow, and dusky apricot accents complimented the basic cream decor. Pots of dwarf palms cast jagged shadows under the track lighting. "Mmmm, nice," she said, looking around her with interest. Through a wall of windows on the far side of the room, the lights of the city of Lafayette sparkled. "Nice view."

"Would you like that drink I promised you to lure you up here?" Julian asked as he moved to the bar behind the sofa.

"Please. A little soda. I'm driving, remember." Nikki was pleasantly tired from dancing. She sank onto a chair and propped her bare feet on the edge of the cocktail table. "I suppose I should feel nervous, visiting the lion in his lair, so to speak," she mused.

"And that's a deliberately provocative observation, if I've ever heard one." He flicked her a challenging glance. "You're only here because you know that I'll play by the rules of the game." His deep voice was as seductive as a caress.

A slow smile curved Nikki's mouth. She tilted her head back, watching Julian through half-closed eyes.

He seemed to have genuinely enjoyed the festival. And his easy manner had allowed her to relax with him. He was still dangerously attractive, but she wouldn't worry about that right now. Not when he was looking at her like that. His gray eyes, alight with banked fires, moved over her lazily. "I think you play by the rules," she commented. "I wonder if you don't make some of them up as you go along."

Julian only smiled. He opened a cabinet on the far side of the bar and the lights dimmed. Music from a light rock station filled the air.

"Or maybe," Nikki went on thoughtfully, "you plan to give me absolute control until I have you just where you want me?"

"Absolutely," he agreed. He gave her the glass of soda and sat in the chair beside hers. He casually propped his bare feet beside her smaller ones.

Nikki sipped her soda and admired his well-shaped toes over the top of the glass. Without even realizing she was doing it, she slid her foot across his and caught one of the dark hairs sprinkled over the top of his foot between two of her toes and tugged it.

"Ouch!" Julian yelped. "*Couillon!*"

Nikki laughed. "Where on earth did you hear that?"

"That's what the lady in the pink jeans called her jitterbug partner when he landed her in the mud." He rubbed the injured foot with the other and cast her a sidelong glance.

"Oh, yeah," she smiled. Her slender foot moved to help administer first aid. "I had a great time."

"You're sure?" His mustache twitched. "I mean, I had decided that I could threaten you with telling Eulalie DesHotels how your bed *really* got broken if it looked like things weren't going well tonight—just to make you more comfortable." His foot forgot that it was the injured appendage as it began a very sensual exploration of Nikki's.

"I haven't danced so much in ages," she said. "It was fun."

"Even the Ferris wheel?" he asked dryly.

"Nothing's perfect."

"No, nothing," Julian agreed, turning his attention to his drink. His mind was on his toes, however, and their sensuous dance.

"Oh!" Nikki sat up, wide-eyed as Julian's toes discovered the sensitive hollow beneath her high arch, which was extremely ticklish. "There goes the radio station!" she exclaimed. "That one goes off the air at midnight." Nikki forcefully jerked her foot from between his and jumped to her feet.

"Coward!" he called after her. As he surveyed her rounded backside in the well-fitting jeans and her unconsciously provocative walk as she moved to the stereo, he decided that he needed a refill. This time as he filled his drink, he didn't cut the bourbon with water, he merely added ice.

Nikki didn't return to her chair, but sat on the sofa. Julian sat beside her. So far, so good, she decided. Then he seemed to develop a fascination for the cubes of ice in his glass.

She felt painfully awkward. She wanted very much for him to kiss her. But she knew he wouldn't break his own rules. He'd give her only as much as she asked. Asking, she decided, could be a damned awkward business.

Plucking up her courage, Nikki reached out, took the glass from his strong hands, and set it aside. Her fingers trembled slightly as she let go of the glass.

Julian looked at her questioningly. Then she saw a

look of stark hunger tighten his features as he realized what she was doing and her heart raced.

She couldn't know that he read the sudden apprehension in her eyes, or that he consciously tempered his reaction, resisting the need to yank her to him and possess her mouth. She reminded him of a kitten he'd once rescued as a boy from a Houston construction sight. Half-starved, it would come near when he coaxed it, and sit with dignity, grooming dusty black fur and regarding him with large, mistrusting eyes. It wouldn't come near enough for him to touch it. He'd eventually captured it in his shirt, collecting several painful scratches and a bite. He'd taken it home, and for weeks he'd fed it and tried to gentle it. But it had never learned to trust him. Maybe Nikki would learn to trust him enough to share what the unbelievably strong chemistry between them promised would be very special. He'd made a promise to himself not to rush her. He placed his hands around her waist.

He held very still as her fingers splayed into the short crisp hair at the back of his head. She delighted in the tactile pleasure of running her fingers through it, so in contrast to the velvety softness she felt as her thumbs traced the outer ridges of his ears. Her fingers moved almost shyly over his forehead, tracing the slight line which divided it and his thick dark brows. They touched his temples and moved like whispers over his closed lids and lashes. They slipped along his strong cheekbones, then down the line of his smoothly shaven jaw to his chin and the slight depression there. Her questing fingers moved to his squared bottom lip and he sucked her finger into his mouth.

With a gasp of surprise, she jerked her hand away.

"Don't stop!" The words were out before he could catch them. He heard her release her breath in a sigh.

He held still, painfully waiting for her to withdraw completely. As her hands slipped back around the strong column of his neck and guided his mouth down to meet hers, he was filled with a surging joy.

Julian stifled an exultant cry. Her mouth was warm and mobile and sweet as he took it hungrily, and she returned his kiss with rising passion, molding her lush curves to him in an act of trust. Then Nikki's tongue slipped into his mouth and he moaned with reaction as his blood took flame. As his tongue met hers, it was Nikki's turn to moan. His bold thrusts left her helpless. Her lips seemed to swell and soften; her mouth opened more, inviting him to deeper penetration.

"My God," Julian groaned into her mouth. The rumble of it vibrating in his deep chest communicated itself to her sensitized breasts, hardening the peaks.

Nikki's hands were on his broad shoulders as she clung to him weakly. How could anything be so devastating? "I feel like I can't get close enough," she whispered in wonder. "Julian, I want to be closer."

Julian drew back from her slightly, bringing a little moan of protest to her lips as his gaze swept her face. His strong hands cupped her face and his mouth swooped down, claiming hers once again, briefly, before he shifted her position, pulling her onto his lap.

Nikki sucked in her breath as she felt his muscular thighs beneath her, felt his male heat and the hardness of his arousal pressing against her thigh. She turned to him, her eyes passion-drugged, her arms finding their way around his neck. Then Julian was kissing her again with tender savagery. His fingers splayed over her supple back, pressing her to him as if he would absorb her, whole, into himself. This was why she'd fought a small war within herself and accepted his invitation for a nightcap, Nikki realized in an instant of stark self-honesty. She had wanted to experience again what she'd tasted before in his arms, to know what this man could give her that no other man had. She had to wonder if the deep response he evoked within her meant that she was now capable of responding to any man that attracted her. Maybe, some feminine instinct told her. But not like this. No, this man was special, from the humor that often danced in those light gray eyes, to his startling perceptiveness. It was only because he'd assured her of complete control that she could feel this free. And what they shared was magical. It had to be. Nothing before had ever felt like this. Then coherent thought spun away as Nikki was carried to a place where there was no sense of future. Or past. No vulnerability in trusting another person to meet her needs. No danger that she would be crushed into submission.

After a small eternity, Julian broke off his deep, drugging kisses. His lips caressed the corner of her mouth then feathered kisses along the line of her jaw until he found the throbbing pulse beneath the point. His tongue traced it and began to move in lazy circles over the sensitive skin of her throat. A curious melting sensation began in her breasts and rushed downward to the core of heat growing at her very center, leaving her weak. "Julian, what you do to me!" she breathed. "I never felt . . . never . . ."

Nikki's gasped words filled him with a fierce tenderness—and a driving need to fill her with himself, to give her the ecstasy of being totally a woman. Her arms pulled him back toward her mouth, but he turned and caught her lobe between his teeth, his warm hand sliding up her jeans-clad thigh. "I want to touch you," he murmured, and felt her shiver in response.

"Please . . ."

His hand cupped her womanhood through her jeans,

and she arched involuntarily backward, against his supporting arm. Her breath came in pants as tremor after tremor of sensation arced through her.

Nikki didn't know how she'd come to be lying on the sofa. Julian slowly stroked the inside of her thighs with his palms until his thumbs met at the apex. His hands went beneath her, lifting her to him, and her head arched back into the cushions. She burned with sensation.

Julian moved up her, untied the knot of her overshirt with unsteady fingers, pushed her tank top above her breasts, unhooked the front clasp of her bra. Her breasts sprang free, and his mouth closed over one taut peak.

Nikki's hand gripped his dark head urging him to deepen the golden assault of his lips and tongue, until she realized that his hand was at the waist of her jeans, tugging them open, and her hands went to his shoulders, her fingers curling uncertainly into his hard flesh.

His skillful fingers found the well of liquid heat at her center, and her head arched backward again, another moan keening from deep in her throat. Julian captured her cry in his mouth as he began rocking his aroused manhood against her thigh to the same rhythm that his fingers were moving. He kissed her, and Nikki again left the world of coherent thought to a place of pure sensation. She began to move against his hand. Her fingers raked down his wide back and caught at his tight buttocks, pressing him more tightly against her.

"Yes!" Julian ground out breaking contact with her mouth for an instant. "This is what I want from you, Nikki. This, and more!"

Her hands moved of their own accord to the ribbed edge of his polo shirt and slipped beneath, up the banded muscles of his torso to the very masculine hardness of his pectorals. Short nails curled into his flesh like little cat's claws as her thumbs found his flat male nipples. They instantly drew up into little beads. Nikki felt his rhythm falter as his body stiffened. She wanted to give him as much pleasure as he was giving her. She moved wantonly against him. It was the first time she'd ever done anything so bold. Bob had hated any show of aggressiveness.

"No!" The cry was ripped from deep within him as Julian jerked away, lifting himself on stiffened arms. For an instant he was utterly rigid, his eyes black, his face a twisted mask. Then his vision cleared. And his heart lurched as he took in the stricken expression in Nikki's deep violet eyes.

"No!" Julian made a helpless, negating gesture with his head, his features still tight. "No, love!" He scooped her resisting form to him and prayed that she should hold still until he had regained some control. "You don't understand," he rasped. "Something was about to happen that hasn't happened to me involuntarily since I was sixteen and having erotic dreams about my biology teacher."

Nikki, relieved, sighed against the curve of his neck, some of the tension leaving her shoulders. "My biology teacher was bald and at least fifty," she mumbled against his warm skin.

"Miss Cranston had flame red hair, and she, too, was at least fifty—the buttons on her lab coat always looked in imminent danger of popping," Julian told her unsteadily as his breathing began to return to normal.

"How . . . ?" Nikki began hesitantly. "I mean . . . we weren't . . ."

Julian felt a rueful smile curve his mouth. "Sex, my dear, is ninety percent in the mind. I was letting mine run wild, and where you are concerned I seem to have a rather, ah, *forceful* imagination."

"Oh . . . Oh!" She suddenly understood.

Julian held her to him and gently stroked her back. He cursed himself for ten kinds of fool. Nikki was so very special. So very fragile. She'd only just begun to build some confidence in herself, and now . . . He remembered her stricken expression and bitterly regretted the damage he'd done. He should have known better; he should have had more control. He'd only been conscious of how much he'd wanted her.

And he still wanted her.

He lay back on the sofa, pulling Nikki with him. She curled into his warmth, her head nestling in the hollow of his shoulder. She felt his fingers idly curl and uncurl in her hair. The music of a piano sonata sculpted the air with sound as silence grew between them.

Nikki closed her eyes and stifled an urge to cry in frustration. He *had* frightened her. Julian's face, harshly twisted by desire, had reminded her of Bob on their wedding night. He'd said that he'd been too excited to stop or to be gentle. Later, there hadn't been any pain. There had only been a wealth of disappointment.

Julian would never callously hurt her, she knew that. He'd given her the space she'd needed to rediscover her own sensuality. She'd wanted this man with a hunger more powerful than she'd ever imagined that she could feel for anyone—all gone in an instant of stark fear.

Now, she ached to ease the storms she sensed still raged within him. But it was a bridge that she just couldn't cross. Not yet.

Nikki snuggled closer, like a child seeking comfort. And Julian, feeling her warm body pressing against him, couldn't help thinking about the wide bed in the bedroom and how it would be to lay her down in it.

And he could.

The thought slipped smooth as satin into his mind. His male instinct told him that he could seduce her— even if she wasn't emotionally ready. He disentangled his fingers from the living silk of her hair.

"I guess we both have early days tomorrow," he said, his voice gruff with unfamiliar emotion.

"I was thinking the same thing."

As she slipped back into her shoes in the hall, he poured his watery drink down the bar sink and splashed himself a finger of straight bourbon and downed it, neat. "I'll walk you down." He didn't bother with his boots.

After unlocking her car, he placed the keys in her hand and folded his fingers over hers, pulling her close. He rested his forehead against hers and said softly, "Thank you for tonight, Nicole. I . . . being with you was very special. Take care driving home."

Nikki stood back and looked up into his shadowed face, looking for that teasing light that she'd come to think was for her alone. At what she saw, something cool slipped along her spine. "Call me?" she asked, touching his lean cheek impulsively.

"I have your number." *Coward. Why don't you tell her you're not sure you can be with her and not do something to hurt her? That you need time to think about things? While you're at it, admit that she's fast becoming too necessary in other ways, and that bothers the hell out of you.*

As Nikki pulled her car into the flow of traffic on Pinhook Avenue, Julian Archer stood in bare feet watching her go and wished he had admitted to her that he wouldn't be calling.

SIX

Nikki paced restlessly over the Oriental rug before the sofa. The radio played softly in the background, a ballad of some sort. Sad. The male singer's poignant voice rose and fell but Nikki was barely aware of anything but her own restlessness.

Damn him.

It had been over two weeks since the Crawfish Festival. Since she'd last seen Julian Archer. He'd promised to call. Or had he? Nikki tried to remember what, exactly, he had said as she left that night. Maybe she had misunderstood.

Maybe she'd misunderstood a lot of things.

But she couldn't have been wrong about what was developing between them. It had been more to him than a casual flirtation, hadn't it? Hadn't he denied his own desires to be sure it was what she wanted?

Nikki crossed her arms as a shiver ran through her. Maybe Julian had gotten tired of waiting for her to decide? she thought bitterly. Life was just a series of games to the man. The pace of this one, evidently, had been too slow.

Or maybe he'd decided he didn't want to be involved with a woman so . . . incomplete.

Nikki paced to the bay window. Her brass easel stood empty, reminding her of a stack of unused canvases in the closet. Her fingers itched with the urge to paint, to put all the anger and frustration on canvas in loud splashes of color.

Past failures held her back. That way lay only more disappointment, more frustration. She turned away.

The phone rang, startling her. She looked at it as though surprised to see it there on the table. She dropped onto the sofa and picked up the receiver. "Hello." Her voice was gruff and irritable.

"Hello, Nikki." The low baritone sent chills up her spine. She sat up stiffly, her feet thudding to the floor.

"Julian . . ." She was suddenly tongue-tied.

"How have you been?" Was there a weariness in his tone?

Why the hell was he calling her now, after more than two weeks? "I'm fine, Julian." She tried to make her voice nonchalant. "How are things in Houston?"

"Busy." The one word spoke volumes. "But I plan to take some time off. And I'd like to see you."

Better late than never? Not hardly. Nikki's heart thumped in her chest as a wave of anger swept over her. Spitting retorts spun through her mind one after the other. Nikki stared mutely at the receiver, wishing it could transmit emotion unspoken.

"Nikki?"

"Yes. I'm still here." She marveled at the flatness of her voice.

"The Bolshoi Ballet is opening in New Orleans this weekend. *Romeo and Juliet*. A business associate of mine had two extra tickets he's willing to trade for a free ride down there in my jet. I thought of you. The

performance is Friday night.'' There was silence for a
moment. ''Well, would you like to go?''

Feelings warred inside Nikki. The Russian ballet.
Julian Archer. New Orleans—*home*. Her head was a
battlefield.

Nikki picked up the phone, stood up, and paced the
floor in front of the sofa. The movement seemed to
quiet the thoughts railing in her mind. Friday night?
Thank God, there was no question of her going; she
had to work. A new compressor was going in at Indian
Point Friday, and it would probably require babysitting
throughout the night.

''I don't think so, Julian. I love the ballet, but I'm
afraid I have to work.'' It *was* a legitimate excuse. The
idea of being in New Orleans with Julian set her teeth
on edge.

''Nikki, there's no one else I want to bring. Please
reconsider.''

Nikki went over in her head the reasons she shouldn't
go. He made her feel too vulnerable. What made him
think that he could just sweep into her life, tumble her
feelings around, then disappear for weeks and now want
her company again? What was worse, she wanted to
see him again. Nicole Colomb, you aren't going to do
this, are you?

''I can't promise you anything. Pop may not be able
to do without my help.''

''Do you want me to call—?''

''No!'' Nikki cut in abruptly. ''I'll take care of it.''
A sudden thought occurred to her. ''Won't we be leaving New Orleans rather late Friday night?''

''I booked a suite at a hotel for the weekend. I
thought that while we were in your city, you might
show it to me the way it should be seen.''

''A suite. Separate rooms?''

"Yes." Julian's tone was neutral.

Nikki pondered the possibilities and a warm flush rose through her body till her cheeks felt hot. She sat down quickly. "All right, if I can get away." She could hardly believe she was saying it. "What time?"

"Can you meet me at the Lafayette Airport at three? That'll give us time to have a light supper and change clothes before the performance," he said. Then added in a softer tone, "I'm looking forward to being with you, Nikki. By the way, have you had a chance to do any dusting?"

What in the world . . . ?

After she'd hung up, Nikki berated herself. Just what are you letting yourself in for, girl? she chided. Haven't you let him get too close already? But the thought of just five minutes with him had her pulse racing and a curious little quickening sensation in her abdomen. There was no question that he excited her, and no one had ever done that before—not like this. But there was something else, too. Something dangerous to her peace of mind. Maybe Pop could give her a reprieve from the decision she was already beginning to regret.

But Pop was pleased to let her off—almost too pleased. "Aw, *cher,* don't worry yourself at all," he said when she called moments later. "The mechanics'll be there for that Jonas job in the Bay. You go and have a good time."

She could call Julian back and tell him she'd changed her mind. She should. She didn't need to make petty excuses. The choice was up to her. And she'd made it. Admit the truth, you want to see him. To be with him. You've never known another man like him, and you may never again.

"Gather ye rosebuds while ye may." The words of a cavalier poet came into her head.

She and Julian moved on two different planes. It would be foolish to think in terms of a lifetime. But, Nikki decided, what they had wouldn't flounder because she couldn't accept a mature relationship. She would gather her rosebuds. Later, she'd have the memories.

After hanging up, Julian stood up from the large oak desk in the center of his office, and walked over to the glass wall that looked out over downtown Houston. He looked down on the streets where the traffic was weekend light. Funny how he always seemed to retreat to his office when things weren't going well, even on Sundays.

And things hadn't been going well. The dent that Grimes had made in the company's funds had been relatively insubstantial. What troubled him now was that he no longer knew who he could trust. He'd taken to questioning things that he usually trusted to others, and it bugged the hell out of him.

And then there was Nikki. Something about the way she was denying her talent disturbed his sense of "rightness." No, he thought. That wasn't all there was to it. She fascinated him. Her softness. Her incredible insight, which was revealed in her paintings. She captured secret dreams. And revealed some of her own.

He walked over to the wall across from his desk where the small oil painting hung, displayed under a special light. There was something so compelling about this picture. The hunter and his dog were crossing a meadow in the hazy, golden sunshine of late afternoon. Beyond them was a copse of trees, and something there had caught both the man and his animal's attention. Something in the deep shadows, there, just out of view. He yearned toward it, trying to pick out detail from the foliage. If he could just make out what it was—he felt like some secret would be revealed to him. Maybe the secret of why a tall woman with dark red-brown hair was becoming so special to him.

Nikki. She had haunted him for two weeks. Exactly like a ghost. She came to him in his sleep, in the middle of executive conferences, when he was doing paperwork.

Julian had decided that enough was enough yesterday when he had discovered that his lunch had gotten cold while he sat at his paper-covered desk trying to work. He had seen her standing there as real as any object in the room. But there had been moonlight in her dark hair and on her bare skin. He didn't know how long he'd sat there, oblivious to his cooling meal and the already neglected backlog of papers. When he'd noticed what was happening, he'd called Daphne, a casual acquaintance he sometimes dated. At dinner he kept seeing Nikki's face transposed on Daphne's. And when Daphne occasionally owned her own face, he found her not only boring, but totally unappealing. When the evening had ended at her apartment with an invitation to spend the night, he'd found the prospect distasteful. Begging off, he'd gone home to his empty bed and a sleepless night.

He'd shown up at the office at six a.m., bleary eyed and glowering. The usually voluble security guard beat a hasty retreat after one look at Julian's face. After a miserable morning of unsuccessful distractions, he had finally given in—given up—and realized that Nikki was in his blood.

He'd even been surprised at how apprehensive the phone call had made him. No, he decided, nothing could surprise him about his relationship with Nikki.

After hanging up the phone, Nikki resolutely grabbed a dust cloth and a can of spray wax off of a shelf in the kitchen closet. What the hell had Julian Archer meant about dusting? She vaguely remembered another comment about her housekeeping sometime earlier. She enjoyed keeping her house up. So what if she'd been a little slack the last couple of weeks? And how did he know?

Nikki attacked the antique cherry wood occasional table that stood against the wall in the living room. The oak dinette was next and all the chairs. When she got to the beautiful built-in library unit that had been part of the room when she'd moved it, her hand lovingly smoothed the rich wood finish. The shelves were filled with her favorite books and a few porcelain and brass keepsakes and gifts. She gently dusted each item, running the cloth over the tops and fronts of the books. The shelves reached all the way to the high ceiling, so she pulled up a chair to climb on.

On the second highest shelf was a tiny figurine of a child. The little girl held an umbrella in one hand and held the other out, palm up, to test for rain. There was an expectant look on her face. Under the figurine was a piece of paper. When Nikki turned it over she saw that it was a check. For five thousand dollars. From Julian Archer.

Nikki stepped shakily down from the chair. She held the check between the fingers of both hands as though trying to make sure it really existed.

Slowly, her addled brain came back to life. This was what the allusions to her dusty house had been about. But what was the check for?

Nikki looked closer at the piece of paper. The loose scrawl was barely legible. It was apparently from his personal account. In the lower left corner of the check was a notation: "One oil painting."

Painting? Nikki stared around her. She had temporarily forgotten about the painting. His choice had surprised her. He had taken the wooded scene with the man and his dog out hunting. She had finished it shortly before Bob's death. Her professor had been especially pleased with it, although she'd never been able to understand why. She'd found that she missed it. But he'd asked if he could take a painting—and she'd given him carte blanche. He'd left her this check that night—or maybe the next morning when he'd come to fix the broken bed.

The check was for her art work. But five thousand dollars? Those high figures were gallery prices for works by well-known artists. She knew she had had potential. Once. Did he really think her painting was that good?

She hugged the check to her. She'd take this to the kids at the Duval House.

The Rolls Royce pulled to a stop in front of the theater on Rampart Street. The uniformed driver ran around to the passenger's side and held the door open to the large back seat. One slender foot appeared. The parking attendant on duty watched with interest as a moire-slippered foot touched the pavement and balanced on the four-inch heel. After it, appeared a long, shimmering, very shapely leg that seemed to go on forever. The woman to whom it was attached was also nicely rounded, he noted with approval as she stood.

Rising from the car to stand behind Nikki, Julian Archer glowered at the fascinated parking attendant, causing the man to hastily find other interests. What could she have been thinking about, wearing a dress slit up to *there*, Julian thought in exasperation. The thigh-high slit closed as she straightened. She probably hadn't realized just how it would look as she moved in it when she'd bought it, he decided. At least—he forced his eyes to safer territory—the jacket was more demure. As he recognized the designer, his lips curled in a self-satisfied smile; she'd probably spent the whole check he'd left on it.

As Nikki turned to catch something Jay Bourque was saying, Julian couldn't help but appreciate the picture she made in the white water-silk dress. That damned slit aside, she showed excellent taste. The fitted jacket had a boat neckline trimmed in a fluttery white fur, which made him want to touch its softness, and let his fingers stray to her warm skin. Tiny buttons fastened it to the waist, where it was gathered into a skirt-like peplum. The fitted sleeves hugged her supple arms and more of that enticing fur circled her wrists. The skirt of the dress underneath hugged her hips lightly, and the heavy fabric rustled as she walked. As their party moved inside, he watched in fascination as the whirls and spirals in the fabric changed with each movement, catching the light.

For a woman who spent a great deal of her time in a hard hat, she carried herself with a natural elegance, he thought. Her hair, with its mahogany highlights, swung like a blunt curtain as she turned her head to look about the lobby.

"Nikki?" A high strident voice rose above the polite murmur of a crowd as the two couples began ascending the stairs. A short woman with a mass of curly brown hair perched atop her head like a rampant birdnest waved a slender arm laden with bracelets.

Nikki groaned softly. It was Beatrice.

Julian glanced down at Nikki questioningly. From the apologetic look she returned, he guessed that this wasn't one of her favorite people. He gazed in amazement as the tiny woman parted the sea of humanity before her to cross the room to where he and Nikki stood.

"Nikki, darling. Where have you been keeping yourself? We haven't seen you in ever so long."

Nikki turned a long-suffering look heavenward and bent to accept the inevitable cheek kiss. She noted wryly that Beatrice's gaze had moved to Julian almost at once. Ah, so that was it. Trust Beatrice to take her opportunities wherever she found them. "Just ever so long," she agreed. "Not since your fourth wedding— or was that your fifth, darling?"

Beatrice looked slightly put out. "Fourth, dear. I haven't had my fifth—" her eyes strayed to Julian, "—yet."

Julian smiled down on the newcomer, who was gazing at him with blatant interest. "A friend of yours, Nikki?"

"No," she answered blandly, "a cousin."

Julian's mustache twitched as the woman's patent smile faltered, then after a glance at Nikki's innocent expression, reasserted itself.

"Beatrice DuMont. Julian Archer." Nikki barely suppressed a giggle which rose from her chest as she saw Beatrice's eyes widen at the name, then take on a hungry sparkle. Beatrice barely managed a polite nod in the direction of the Bourques as Nikki introduced them.

Julian was enjoying the strange undercurrents between these two. He was fascinated that this brassy, heavily-perfumed brunette was related to Nikki.

"Beatrice, I think I see your escort over there trying to get your attention." Nikki indicated a wildly gesticulating man on the other side of the plush lobby. "We wouldn't want to keep you."

The pouty, disappointed look her cousin threw her

was almost more than Nikki's self-control could take. "Of course. But, Nikki, dear, please do come by while you're in town. And bring Julian with you, of course."

"Of course," Nikki echoed as Beatrice moved reluctantly away to rejoin her date. Then, under her breath, "When pig's fly."

The sparkle in Julian's eyes revealed that he'd heard. But it quickly vanished and the invisible curtain he'd maintained between them ever since she'd boarded the plane in Lafayette dropped back into place. Nikki resisted the urge to kick his shin.

"Do you have many relatives in New Orleans?" Lena Bourque asked.

"Hundreds," Nikki replied dryly, thinking that Beatrice fit in with the rest very well.

The lights blinked, signaling that the performance was about to begin. Julian graciously offered Lena his arm. Nikki accepted Jay's with a smile. An usher guided them to their box.

Nikki found herself seated in the front of the box with Lena. Julian was seated above and behind her right shoulder, with Jay seated at the same angle behind Lena. Nikki had a wonderful view of the stage, but as the lights dimmed and the overture began, her mind was on the tall man behind her.

The evening was not progressing as she had imagined it would during her shopping trip to an exclusive designer boutique, which catered to Lafayette's oil wealthy. There, she had gone slightly mad. Now she felt like a surprise package waiting to be unwrapped. She glanced at Julian. It would be worth it, she decided, just to wipe that impassive look off his face for an instant, to rip aside that damned curtain of indifference.

"Julian, would you mind helping me take off my jacket? It's a little warm in here."

"Certainly." He stood and Nikki turned to him as she unbuttoned the jacket. There was a certain challenge in her smile. The fur fell aside, revealing a sensually curved hammered gold collar that was almost primitive in design, and which matched the heavy earrings at her lobes. The curves of the heavy necklace just revealed the slight hollow at the base of her throat between her collar bones. Nikki's hands unfastened the tiny row of buttons inside each sleeve. When she had finished, Julian slid the jacket from her shoulders. And caught his breath.

Demure, hell!

"Do you like it?"

"Is that a dress or a serving platter?" His deep voice rumbled near her ear. He couldn't help pausing there to drink in the soft scent of her skin—and there was a great deal of it open to view, too. She looked as if she'd just slipped from the cover of *Cosmo*. The creamy smooth mounds of her breasts, which rose gently with each indrawn breath, were pushed up and nearly exposed by the stiff flare of the bodice, which stood out like a rose petal peeling away from the bud. A cut vee opened between them to where the fabric hugged her ribs, allowing for all kinds of play of light and shadow to hint at that which remained unrevealed. Why, if it weren't for more of that damned fur, which edged the top, he would be able to see—*my God!*

"Julian, you're crushing my jacket." Nikki took it from him. Smoothing the material, she resumed her seat. Julian sat, too. Unfortunately, his height afforded him a marvelous view over Nikki's shoulder. He glanced at Jay, measuring line-of-sight and gave a mental sigh of relief when he realized that Lena blocked Jay's view of Nikki. As his gaze moved to the audience below, he thanked fate that their seats weren't down there.

"That's a marvelous dress," Lena Bourque was saying. "Something about your hair style and that wide gold band on your upper arm makes me think of Cleopatra."

Cleopatra, Julian thought, forcing his gaze to the dancers below. *Mark Antony never stood a chance!*

He focussed his eyes on the stage. But the spectacle below wasn't nearly as appealing as the woman before him. He could imagine the feel of her skin as he stroked her back, the way her hair would fall over her face as she bent over his reclining form to press her eager mouth on his. The message her choice of evening wear sent him was obvious. Stop it! he commanded himself. He'd made a promise to himself and to Nikki—even if she didn't know it. He wasn't going to make love to her.

He remembered the last time they'd been together. Everything had seemed perfect. Nikki had been so incredibly warm. Giving. The memory of what they'd begun to share had the power to make him ache. Then a simple misunderstood signal and her face had gone stark with fear. Some of those shadows in her blue-violet eyes were very, *very* deep.

He couldn't forget that look. Or that he'd harmed her through his selfishness. No, he was going to keep his hands off—even if it killed him. He didn't want to be free of her. He suspected that he was already a permanent captive—the idea made a smile curve Julian's chiseled lips.

"Thank you for this evening, Julian. The performance was wonderful." Nikki looked up into a face that was dark and closed against her. Lena had given her a knowing look as she and Julian had said goodnight to the Bourques. Lena, Nikki decided, had been wrong. She tried once again to understand what was happening between them. It still confused her. The beginnings of a tension headache nagged at her temples.

"I thought you'd enjoy the performance." With a few deft flicks of his fingers, Julian loosened his black tie and opened his collar.

I always enjoy a good performance! Nikki wanted to yell at him. *Would you please explain the one you're giving now?*

Julian moved across the expanse of hunter-green carpet to the telephone on a Louis XIV style desk. The entire suite, with its gold tasseled Austrian drapes and velvet upholstered furniture, smacked of the ostentatious opulence that Nikki found distasteful. "Would you like anything from room service?" Julian asked as he lifted the receiver.

Nikki's eyes caught and held his. She might have begged him to explain what was happening; how he could have changed completely from the person she'd found it so easy to confide in. But her pride forbad it. She wouldn't end things on a sour note. She owed this man a great deal. Whether he understood it or not, he'd helped her to come out of her self-imposed emotional exile and rejoin the human race. She would always be grateful to him for that. A lump formed, blocking her throat. Nikki swallowed it with difficulty. "No, Julian. There's nothing I want." Both knew the statement had nothing to do with his question.

Julian winced at the flat certainty in her voice. "Nicole!"

She turned away and moved toward her room. The set of her shoulders was stiff beneath her loosely draped jacket. "Nikki!" Hard fingers closed over them and spun her around. "I'm sorry. I'm not handling this very well." The words were tense. His grip slackened, but he didn't release her.

"I thought that you were doing marvelously," Nikki bit out. "This *is* the scene where you tell me that I've been an amusing little diversion, but not—"

"Diversion, hell!"

Julian's mouth crushed hers. Nikki's hands went up to push him away as he pressed her against the wall, his body molding itself to her forcefully. But they went around his neck, pulling him even closer.

His fingers cupped her head, clutching her thick hair as he tilted her face to his. As his tongue parted her teeth and slipped inside her mouth, Nikki arched against him, inviting even more. He did want her! she thought exultantly. He wasn't indifferent—and that knowledge stilled her earlier uncertainties as a wild, sweet joy raced through her, even as Julian's hands slipped along her neck and down her sides, creating a warm urgency within her. The urgency grew with swift violence as his hands caressed the flare of her hips.

His hands moved back to her waist and held as Julian drew his mouth from hers. He placed kisses on her cheeks and on her closed lids before resting his forehead against hers with a sigh.

"Tonight isn't going the way I planned," Julian told her raggedly.

"For me, either."

Julian shifted, his gaze drifted down to the top of the dress beneath her unbuttoned jacket. "Yes, well, that's not your fault," he told her ruefully. Then his eyes moved back to Nikki's. Her irises were wide and dark. Her lids with their thick burden of lashes were half-closed. He saw the desire and the invitation in them. He remembered the hurt and confusion that he'd seen in them the last time that they were together, that terrible look that he'd inadvertently caused, and he knew that he couldn't. He couldn't risk harming her.

"Nikki . . ." Julian sucked in a breath and shook his head slightly. Some perversity made him touch the fur edging the top of her gown, letting his fingertips brush across the rise of her breast. His hand dropped and iron control tightened his features.

"Do you trust me enough to do what I ask?"

"Yes." It was barely a whisper.

Julian bent and, for a long instant, pressed his warm lips to where his fingertips had just set her skin afire, feeding the flame. When he straightened, his face was tortured. "Then, please, go to bed."

He reluctantly broke contact between them. Nikki's eyes implored him to say more, to explain. He drew in a shaky breath. "We have to talk. And, tonight, I just don't trust myself. We'll talk tomorrow, I promise."

Nikki nodded slowly. Then, impulsively, she rose to place a kiss on the slight indentation of his chin. "I trust you, Julian."

She went down the short hall to her room without a backward glance.

Julian Archer watched the tip of his cheroot glowing red in the dark, then ground it out irritably. He'd taken advantage of the lateness of the hour to place several overseas calls. Then he'd given an hour and a half to the work he'd brought with him from Houston, clearing most of it.

Julian discarded his shirt studs on the dresser and stripped off his shirt. He rubbed the fatigued muscles at the base of his neck. He was tired but not sleepy. Still in his tuxedo pants, he stretched his long legs out on the bed, propping himself against the rolled-and-tucked velvet headboard. He'd purposely left the bourbon decanter in the sitting room.

A muffled sound from somewhere beyond the wall which divided his room from Nikki's swung his head around. Julian listened closely for several seconds, but all was quiet. He could go to her door and look in, make sure that she was all right. He drew in a deep breath and released it. No. If she were sleeping, he didn't want to disturb her. And if she wasn't? It had already been a trying night for both of them.

Julian smiled into the darkness at the situation he found himself in. Then he tilted his head back, closing his eyes, recalling certain points in the contracts that he'd just gone over.

Another sound—this one a cry—sent him out of bed and running toward Nikki's room.

SEVEN

Julian burst through the door. A shaft of light fell on a writhing, sobbing form. Nikki's voice fell in waves of terror. "Get him off! Oh God! Help me! Get him off!"

When Julian tried to take her in his arms, she began flailing, beating at him with frantic hands. "No! No! Get off me!" The words dissolved into hysterical sobbing.

"Nikki! Nikki! It's me. Julian! I won't hurt you, Nikki. Please wake up!" He tried to sound soothing, but his voice cracked with concern. She pushed at him frantically, eyes wide but unseeing.

"No, Bob! No! I can't." Then her eyes widened in recognition. She slumped against Julian's chest, her body heaving with sobs.

Julian, his face grim, pulled her tighter against him, softly rubbing her back and making deep cooing noises in his throat.

Like floodgates opened after a long rain, the tears poured down her face.

"It was the accident—when Bob died. It keeps coming back!

"We were going down the highway, the one that goes to Bancker Ferry. Bob was so angry! God, he looked like some kind of monster. His face was so red. The veins stood out on his forehead. He was yelling at me." Waves of tremors shook her, and the hiccoughing aftermath of sobs choked her words. Her eyes focused on some terrible event in her mind as tears continued to stream down her face. "It was all my fault. I wanted to continue college—to study art. I couldn't understand why it made him hate me. I can still hear the words. I told him to slow down. He was driving so fast! I told him he couldn't intimidate me into quitting. I was terrified, but I couldn't let him see it. He always used my fear of him.

"God! When he slammed on the brakes going around the curve the seat belt nearly cut me in half. He was drunk—and so mad! I begged him, 'Please.' Oh, God. I can see his face so clearly. He yelled at me again: 'Please? I remember asking you *please*, but you said that you had to do what was right for you.' " She halted. Julian sat very still.

"I shouted back at him that just because we were married didn't mean he owned me! I said, 'I want to study art—that's who *I* am!' But he said, 'You're my wife!' Like that was all I could be. I told him that he'd known what my plans were before we were married— and that I didn't care how much he shouted, or how recklessly he drove—that he wasn't going to bully me into changing my mind." Nikki stopped speaking. Her eyes found Julian's face. "He was so different when we were dating. He seemed kind and understanding. My aunt had died. She'd been the only family I'd known since I was six. I was so depressed. So vulnerable."

Her head fell against Julian's chest again. She felt

so warm and small to him, like a sad little child. He wrapped comforting arms around her.

"I felt so guilty. She died after I went away to college," she continued, her words still punctuated by left-over sobs. "We had a fight before I left. Aunt Rosalie wanted me to go to school in New Orleans where I could be under her thumb. I refused. And then she was gone before we had a chance to patch it up.

"I was alone. When Bob came into my life, he made me feel important to him. I thought he was everything. My Prince Charming. I thought he'd give me everything I needed—love, understanding, support. And for awhile he did.

"Or maybe I just needed that so much that I blinded myself to the demanding side of him." She seemed to be talking to herself, trying to find reasons for what had happened.

"I knew that he'd been bitterly hurt when his injury ended his career. I did everything I could to try to make things easier for him. I lost a semester at school to stay home with him after the joint replacement surgery. But it seemed the more I gave him the more he wanted. I had to stand up for myself." Again, she turned her face up to his, as though looking for affirmation. "I had to start somewhere. And I'd been offered a chance to study in Paris." She shook her head, caught up in the past. She could still hear Bob's voice in her mind: *"Yes, you will quit college if I say so! You can trash that garbage about going to Paris to study, Miss DaVinci! Why don't you come out from behind your paint and canvas long enough to think about what I want for a change? I love you! I want you home at night when I get back from work. You're only studying art, anyway . . . or is it that art professor you're so hot on studying, cher?"*

"He was so unfair. And he kept driving faster and

faster. The truck almost ran off the road, and he took his hand off the wheel to grab my arm because I wasn't looking at him! He screamed at me to answer him! I don't know where I found the nerve to tell him that I was tired of all his shouting. I told him that deciding whether or not to quit college was *my* decision." Nikki's chest heaved with the force of the emotions roiling through her. "I told him I wouldn't give up all my dreams to stay home and kowtow to him.

"He lifted his hand off the steering wheel and drew it back as if he would hit me. The look on his face was horrible. And then, he just turned white and stared at the road. Oh, God! And when I looked out the windshield . . ." Nikki's large amethyst eyes widened as though she were seeing the scene. "It was too late to stop! Bob slammed on the brakes but it was too late! The ferry was on the other side of the river!" The words came out in gasps. "I don't know why I ducked—crouched down over my legs and covered my face with my hands. The truck crashed right through the barrier arm! Glass went everywhere! It was so slow. I could feel us falling forever. Then all of a sudden, water rushed in the broken windshield!" Her voice had gradually gotten louder, panic tinged it again as her tears fell faster.

"The truck kept bobbing! Water kept coming in, and Bob was on top of me! I couldn't get him off me! And I could hear him calling me!" Nikki struggled in Julian's arms, pushing him away.

He pulled her tightly to him. "Nikki! It's over now. It's all over. You got out!" She slowly ceased her struggles as his words got through to her. She quieted, the only movement the tides of shivers that swept her body.

After a few moments she raised her tear-stained face.

With a look of torment that twisted his insides, she said softly, "I got out. But Bob didn't." As though those final words summed up the crushing pain inside her, she began to weep softly.

Julian held Nikki against him and let her cry. As he understood this terrible guilt that she carried—needlessly—he ached to take away her pain. His hands moved involuntarily to her head, one tangling in her dark hair, the other stroking a satiny, tear-dampened cheek. Gradually, she quieted, snuggling into him, rubbing her cheek against the mat of hairs on his chest. Her hands that had been still at his waist, moved slowly to his back.

Julian was suddenly very much aware of the feel of her—her soft tousled hair—her firm breasts pressed against his abdomen. The tenderness within him mixed with a fierce possessiveness and an almost violent passion. She was his now. He would make her his. And he'd see to it nothing ever hurt her again.

Nikki pulled away from Julian's soothing embrace. She lifted her eyes slowly from the lightly furred muscles of his chest up to his strong chin, where his clenched jaw betrayed the tension that possessed him. Her eyes rested on his lips for a moment, then moved upward to meet his eyes.

For a moment she couldn't read the expression in them, couldn't comprehend the great emotion burning there. She looked away for a second, shocked. When she looked back she understood. She saw the depth of his compassion, his caring—his desire.

As she stared at him, her body flared with a need that she had only begun to be aware of these last few weeks. She had to be a part of this man whose eyes burned her and soothed her all at once. With a soft gasp, Nikki pulled Julian to her. She kissed the warm flesh at the base of his throat, trailing little kisses to the place where a frantic pulse beat at the side of his neck.

Julián trembled. He looked down at Nikki in astonishment as she traced kisses to his breast bone. There was almost a reverence in the way her lips touched him. His body rushed to life as he realized that she was freely giving him everything he had wanted from her since the day she had first appeared in Grimes's office. Something, some feeling within him that he had long held in check, burst free.

"Nikki," he rasped out. She lifted her head from where she was tasting his skin, and she smiled. As he looked at her radiant face a tightness banded his chest, as though his heart had swelled or tears were barely contained. He lifted his shaking hands and cupped her face. He pulled those precious lips against his.

Her mouth opened immediately beneath his. But it was not a surrender. As he explored her mouth with his tongue, hers searched his out. And when he withdrew his tongue, hers followed to taste and touch.

Julian slid his hands down over her shoulders to grasp her upper arms. He moved her away from him. Nikki was shocked. Then she saw in his face that it was not the rejection she had instantly feared. The need she saw there was so strong it almost made her look away.

She threw her head back, tossing her hair off her face. She thrust her shoulders back, sitting up straight for his scrutiny. A strange feeling of joy bubbled through her body as she realized, for the first time in her life, that she held a kind of power within her. She felt beautiful. She felt desirable. And she could make this man—this incredible man—want her.

Julian's eyes dilated at the sight of Nikki displaying

her splendor. Her gown of pale blue had obviously been designed to be as tantalizing as possible. Her beautiful breasts were more revealed than concealed by cups of intricate lace. He could see her erect nipples with their wide pink areolas peeking through the lace. Her torso was swathed in blue silk that was so sheer he could almost see the tint of her skin through it. Where her gown had twisted beneath her legs, gores of lace revealed the skin of her thighs. She was . . . incredibly desirable.

And in her eyes he could see that she wanted him, too.

With a groan, Julian took Nikki in his arms. His breath puffed in hot little gusts against her ear, sending shivers through her. With a cry she turned her face to his, and their lips came together. Nikki put all her wanting into that kiss. She wanted to be consumed by his body, and to consume him, too. The force of the feelings trembling through her doubled as the kiss grew stronger, more demanding.

He couldn't get enough of her lips, her mouth. He traced circles over the silk covered skin of her back with his hands. She moved against him as if the feel of it tickled her. He groaned against her teeth as her movements incited him, made him ache to be inside her.

Julian stood abruptly, carrying Nikki with him. Setting her on her feet, he pulled her even closer. He couldn't bear to break the contact between them.

Nikki thrilled to the feel of his hardness against her body. She moved her hands down over his back to his hips, caressing from the powerful ridged muscles of his back to his tight buttocks. When she pulled his hips against her, pressing against his swollen manhood, she felt him throbbing with a passion that matched the pulsing deep within her.

Julian pulled away from her again, not able to take the pressure that brought him so close to losing control. "Nicole . . ." Julian drew a deep lungfull of air. "We have to stop. You don't know what you're doing to me."

"I'm not a child. Of course, I do," she said, her voice husky with emotion. "I want you." She felt a tremor pass through him.

"Nikki . . . I'm not going to make love to you."

"Do you trust me enough to do what I ask?" The familiarity of the question struck, and he realized that it was his own. He nodded, looking into her eyes. They were darkened to indigo by passion.

"Then make love with me, Julian. It's what I want."

He drew in a sharp breath and searched her face, finding there the answer he sought. The last of his resistance dissolved. He pulled her to him, reveling in the feel of her, in the way her body molded itself to him— willingly—actively.

Nikki watched the play of emotion on his strong features. She didn't expect Julian to stay forever. He wasn't that kind of man. But she was very sure that this was right. She had been alone for so long. She had let guilt and fear rule her life—leaving it a sterile, gray, unsatisfying existence. Julian had broken through that barrier somehow, given her the ability to feel again. Deep inside she trusted him, and she wanted more than anything to share this intimacy.

She raised her hands to comb her fingers through the dark hairs that furred his chest. She could feel his breathing quicken, his heartbeat pound harder under her fingers.

Her own heart pounded as his hands moved to her

shoulders, gently smoothing the thin straps of her gown over them and down her arms. The peaks of her breasts caught and held the lace for a moment before it slid free.

Julian's eyes devoured her. She stood straight before him, bathing in that look. She held her breath as his hand slowly rose, pausing for just a moment only centimeters from her skin. For that instant she could feel the heat from his fingers, which were so tantalizingly close. When he touched her, running his index finger along the underside of her breast, up her breast bone and down to trace the curve of the other, she gasped little panting breaths. A flush rose over her body, the heat of it centering on where he touched her—and lower. She had never experienced anything so powerful.

His voice came, gruff with passion. "So beautiful." His hands moved behind her as he pulled her toward him. Her breasts were flattened against him, the hair on his chest creating an exquisite friction. Julian caressed her back and shoulders. His hands felt so warm and smooth against her chilled skin. She shivered.

"Darling . . . Nikki . . . are you cold?" Gooseflesh spread itself over her, but she shook her head.

"No . . . not cold," she whispered. Her arms came up around him and she buried herself in him.

"Come here . . . to the bed." His voice was so rough, as though he could hardly speak. But his eyes glowed as he looked at her. She had that feeling of drowning again, of being consumed by the force of his gaze. She dropped her lids over her eyes to shut it out.

"Nikki!" His hold on her was the only thing that kept her from falling. His expression was startled when she opened her eyes again. "Please . . ." Her knees buckled and she sat on the edge of the bed. Her eyes met the line of hair that trailed from his chest to his navel and downward. She longed to see what was hidden where it disappeared into the waistband of his slacks.

Nikki's hands moved with a will of their own. Her trembling fingers released the band, eased the zipper down its track with a soft hissing sound. When she would have grasped the waistband of his slacks and briefs and pulled them down over his lean hips, Julian grabbed her hands.

"No!" The word came out in an explosion of air. She looked up at him, puzzled. His face, twisted with ardor, softened as he sighed. "If . . . let me do it." He stepped back from her, bent over to ease the clothing to the floor. Then he straightened.

He was magnificent. His proudly held head was capped by hair that looked black in the subdued light. His gray eyes glittered at her, his appraisal as frank as her own. His face was lined, but the marks bespoke strength. Above his incredibly expressive lips his mustache enhanced his features. His neck and shoulders showed the color and muscling that could only have come from hard work in the sun. His chest was firm; his midriff well-delineated. There was only a slight indentation at his waist.

Then Nikki's eyes travelled down his flat belly to the forest of blackness at his groin. She gazed on the proof of his arousal for long seconds, barely able to contain the throbbing excitement that made her long to reach out, touch the taut skin, feel the pulsing heat of him.

She had almost amassed the courage to reach out and stroke the hard thighs when Julian's voice again broke the silence and she looked up at him. "Your turn, Nicole." His smile was like a kiss.

She stood on shaky legs, inches from his compelling

body. His eyes caught and held hers while she pushed the silk gown down over her hips to fall like a pool at her feet. She watched his face as his gaze moved over her, his hungry eyes devouring her.

The beauty of her took his breath from him. The light from the doorway bathed her with a golden glow. Her hair fell dark and shadowing across her face, leaving her eyes lavender points of light. Her soft shoulders and the rosy-tipped mounds of her breasts rose and fell with each puffing breath. Her flat torso narrowed in a waist that looked small enough to span with his hands, then flared into soft hips. Her rounded tummy harbored the tiny cavern of her navel from which a path of hair, almost golden in the light, led to the dark thatch at the juncture of her thighs.

And suddenly, he couldn't just look at her anymore. He swept her into his arms, breathing in her sweet scent as he lay her on the rumpled sheets of her bed. He felt a moment of hesitation and quickly pushed it aside. It was what they both wanted. Her eyes, her hands told him it was. And God, how he wanted her!

He lay down against the length of her, marveling in the silkiness of her. He tangled his hands in her hair, pulled her face to his, sought her mouth, her tongue. He rolled her over atop him and pulled her head back, searched her face, her eyes, finding there a passion to match his own. And when her hands found and held him, he knew that all restraint was gone.

Nikki raised herself slightly above him. Her hair fell forward across her face, and she looked at him through its concealing curtain. His face fascinated her. Its strength. Its intensity. When he smiled it was almost boyish. When his face filled with passion—as now—there was an almost primitive masculinity about it. Her artist's eyes stored all those things away in her memory even while her body flared with each new sensation. She throbbed with the need to be a part of him.

Julian flicked his tongue over the point of one breast. An involuntary moan escaped from her and rose in volume when he drew the tip into his mouth. She closed her eyes, drawn down into the pool of sensation created by his suckling mouth. When he claimed the other, she opened her eyes again to watch him and that primal need increased. When he buried his head between her breasts, she absorbed into herself the feel of his flushed skin, the wet softness of his questing tongue. A deep, fulfilling joy surged through her. She delighted in the feel of him, the musky smell of his heated skin, the moans her touch evoked. She found herself directing his hands, his lips to all her sensitive places. And then she took the final ultimate step. She rose above him, guiding him into the core of her, and gave him the very center of herself.

They moved together, as though one mind drove them. She reveled in the urgency that gathered force in her whole being. For a moment, it all seemed suspended in time as he turned her, moved her onto her back beneath him. Then the inferno resumed its consuming fire until, in an infinite second of glory, the force shattered.

For moments, the strength of that explosion bathed her. A slow awakening to reality came as the pleasure spread through her limbs. Nikki opened her eyes and gazed up at Julian. His expression was a puzzle. His eyes burned with a tenderness that was almost frightening. Their bodies were molded to each other, still joined. Nikki felt so much a part of him. A sharp pain cut through her at the realization that soon they must move apart. But for the moment, she could enjoy this delicious peace, this melding.

Julian watched as Nikki's eyes slowly closed, and a soft smile grazed her lips. A powerful tenderness tightened his chest. He had showed her that being a woman could be beautiful—and that meant more to him than the exquisite pleasure she had given him. Now he would show her that it could only get better. The future would be a world of exploration for them both.

EIGHT

Nikki woke to the sight of a pair of startling gray eyes looking down at her. A grin curved the chiseled lips above her, and her cheeks reddened with the memory of the night before.

"Good morning, beautiful," Julian said, his warm voice rumbling. "I've been waiting for you to wake up." His eyes glinted mischievously as he bent to claim her mouth. The demanding kiss roused her from sleep, and the sudden feel of his body atop hers brought her thoroughly alert. She was completely aware that neither of them were wearing any clothes. As his hands moved sensuously over her, she began to feel slightly off balance.

Dragging her lips from beneath his, Nikki gasped, "Good morning, yourself! Do you always wake up so . . . so . . ."

"Hungry?" he supplied.

"Hungry," she agreed, a little breathless as his warm lips found the point of one shoulder. The soft brush of his mustache was exquisite.

"Actually, I'm ravenous," he said, punctuating his

statement with a low growl. "What about you?" His eyebrows quirked, but he continued his nibbling exploration, descending to the peak of one breast. He slid his hands under her back, arching her up to his questing lips. Nikki moaned softly as he licked the underside of each breast.

"Mmm . . . salty." He grinned. She resisted an impulse to stick her tongue out at him.

"How can anyone be in such a good mood this early in the morning?" she groaned.

"You'll just have to get used to it, I guess." Her response was lost in a fit of giggles as Julian found a ticklish spot on her rib cage with his tongue. The laughter turned to little mews of pleasure as his mouth traveled downward. Her passion-closed eyes suddenly opened wide as she realized what his ultimate destination was.

"Julian!" She wasn't ready to make love again. She needed to sort out her feelings. Last night had been so special, so . . . spiritual. But, now, she needed time.

Julian glanced up, deviltry in his eyes. "Yes?" as his hands slid under her buttocks.

"I'd really like to have a shower first," she pleaded. "I feel like I . . . like . . ."

"Like you've made love all night?" he finished. Her expression pleaded with him to understand.

"Sure," he said. His smile was gentle as he helped her up from the bed, openly admiring what was revealed before she dragged the sheet around her.

What had happened between them last night had been so powerful that she needed a chance to examine it by daylight. She was relieved when he turned her toward the bathroom and gave her a swat on the bottom to send her on her way.

The pulsing spray of the shower felt luxuriant. Nikki

tilted her head back beneath it, watching clouds of steam floating upward, filling the black-and-white tiled bathroom.

Like that water turning to steam, she felt different from herself. Strangely fragmented. Changed. The memory of Julian's passion returned to her in a rush and an echo of what they'd shared shivered through her. It had been almost too beautiful. Too perfect. Nothing in her life before had prepared her. . . . She felt as if she must gather the pieces of herself back together quickly, before the sheer force of Julian's personality and the intensity of what they shared scattered those pieces forever.

Oh, he wouldn't harm her intentionally, Nikki knew that. He was sincere in what he felt, he truly desired her and enjoyed her company. But a game was only fun until it was mastered. And last night had been a victory of sorts.

No, he'd never deliberately hurt her. He'd simply lose interest over time.

She just needed space to catch her breath, Nikki decided as she pulled back a little out of the spray and measured shampoo into the cup of her palm. She needed to reestablish autonomy with herself. It would be so tempting to relax and be swept away. But would it only last until the first white-hot fire of desire cooled? Yes. She wanted more than that. However, she was realistic enough not to believe in happily-ever-after.

She reminded herself that some things just weren't possible, no matter how much one wanted them, so it was important to take what one could have.

Nikki closed her eyes, tilting her head back beneath the spray to rinse away the suds, enjoying the feel of the water. She wasn't so submerged, however, that she wasn't aware of a slight draft of cool air at the opening of the shower door, or of the shadow which came between her closed lids and the light.

"Julian Archer!"

"You were expecting someone else, perhaps?"

Nikki couldn't prevent a smile, and as his hands circled her waist and slipped upward, she caught her breath. "You look wonderful in water," he murmured.

Nikki blinked her eyes clear of water and found Julian looking down at her with such warm intensity that a shiver traced along her spine. Heat bloomed deep within her and spiraled outward.

"I decided that I wanted a shower, too." The movement of his fingers as they played in the water, sluicing along her spine, weren't those of a man anxious to grab the soap. Nikki reached for the bar and lathered the hair on his chest, then felt it slip from her fingers.

"One should always be careful in the bath," Julian breathed near her ear as her breasts slid deliciously against his soapy chest. "Statistics show that seventy-five percent of all household accidents happen in the bathroom." Then his hand slipped further down, and she arched her back, pressing more tightly against him.

"Oh, yes!" The words were lost under his consuming lips.

"How can anyone possibly eat that much this early in the morning?" Nikki asked, eyeing the hearty breakfast on Julian's plate. Mounds of scrambled eggs were crowded to one side of his plate by sausage, hash browns, bacon, and biscuits.

"I told you that I was ravenous. Besides, I have to keep up my strength," he answered, with an exaggerated waggle of his eyebrows. "Breakfast is the most important meal of the day. I love it when you blush."

Nikki pretended to ignore him, dipping her spoon

into the bowl of fresh fruit that was her breakfast. As she bit into a slice of peach, her eyes traveled around the room.

The Rain Forest was one of the highlights of the huge Hilton Hotel in New Orleans. A large expanse of windows looked down over the river and parts of the downtown area. The tables lined the windows and banks of planters throughout the lounge and soft music played as a background. She started as a flash of light caught her eye, and smiled to herself as thunder rumbled beneath the music.

Julian looked up in surprise as another lightning flash came. A second later a crack of thunder split the air. The music faded as the calls of tropical birds filled the room. The sound of rain falling caused him to look around. He frowned. Outside the sky was clear, and the sun beamed, a perfect spring day. Suddenly, water began to fall like a tropical shower on the lush plants in the banks of acrylic planters all around the restaurant and the significance of the lounge's name struck him.

Julian looked at Nikki, who was just barely concealing a facetious smile. "Interesting atmosphere," he said. "I almost expect to see monkeys swinging over my head." He glanced at the ceiling.

"It should suit you perfectly. I half expected you to put on a loincloth this morning and beat your chest," she told him, eyebrows raised.

He chuckled. "Me? Tarzan?" Nikki groaned. He was still as attractive as if he had been dressed in a loincloth, she thought, noticing how his chest-hugging polo shirt and khaki slacks showed off his athletic physique.

Julian's mind was occupied with a problem that had suddenly come to him as he had dressed. For the first time since he'd been a teenager, he'd forgotten to use protection. He had come on this trip prepared, but the suddenness of what had happened between him and Nikki had blown all caution from his mind. Now, the possible consequences of that omission were racing through his mind. He'd have to find a way to bring up the subject with her later. He wanted to assure her that, no matter what happened, he would be there with her to see it through. But it would have to be the right time. For now, he'd just enjoy spending the day with her. "Okay, what other surprises do you have in store for me today?"

"Me?"

"Yes. This is your city. I want you to be my personal tour guide."

Nikki thought about it for a moment as she took the last sip of her coffee. The idea appealed to her. It had been a long time since she'd really explored New Orleans. Showing it to Julian would be like taking a fresh look at familiar surroundings.

"I have to make a call first," Nikki told him. "Then I'll play tour guide. There are phones in the lobby. Let's go." Julian was curious. But didn't pry.

Later, when she rejoined him after the call, her eyes were troubled. "I have a stop to make before we start our tour," she told him. "The streetcars run out that way, if you'd like to come along."

"Where are we going?" he asked her as they rode one of the quaint cars, enjoying the view down Saint Charles Street in the garden district. With a clang of its bell the car stopped at each corner or when a passenger pulled the cord.

"It's not far," Nikki said. Julian didn't notice that she had avoided his question. They passed large, beautifully landscaped homes along the shady street. After they passed Audubon Park, the area became less affluent.

After a few more stops, Nikki pulled the cord and they got off the street car. Large oak trees still shaded the sidewalks. A white elephant of a house loomed before them. A small sign near the front door read, "DUVAL HOUSE."

Julian turned to Nikki. "Your home?"

"At one time," she said. Her expression was carefully shielded.

He studied the neo-Greek architecture, married unhappily to French and Spanish influences. It must have once been quite a showplace—incongruous though the style was. It had apparently gone to seed a bit over the years.

Julian looked back at the woman beside him. "What is it, a museum?" he asked.

Her face broke into a smile he didn't understand. "Used to be." She laced her fingers through his and led him up the walk. "Now my kids live here."

"Kids?" Julian studied her in surprise. "I didn't know you had children. You've never mentioned them."

She gave him a wide-eyed look. "Oh, yes. Lots of them." They opened the door to pandemonium. High-pitched laughter and the sound of running feet accompanied the blaring of a rock song. Julian watched with amazement as at least half a dozen small bodies flashed by him, one after the other. As he took a step forward, a small red-haired boy whizzed by in midair after flying off the end of the banister. Instinctively, Julian reached out and grabbed a handful of jeans and belt and set the child safely on his feet. When a little girl appeared from a doorway on the right, thumb in mouth and clutching a faded stuffed rabbit, he knew something was up. The child's face was dark as teak and her eyes like little ebony stones. She looked up at Julian with wide fearful eyes, backing away slowly.

"It's okay, Keely. He's a friend." With infinite gentleness, Nikki stroked the child's head. She looked up at Julian who was staring at her with an expression of dawning comprehension.

"Your kids, huh? How many do you have?"

Nikki's eyes twinkled with mirth. "Oh, about forty-eight or so. It changes from week to week."

His reply was forestalled by two boys of about ten hurtling down the banister, and the noise of running steps above his head. He made as if to grab the boys as they made their getaway, and growled, "That's enough! No more sliding down the banister!" He was startled by a sudden burst of crying from the little girl near Nikki.

Nikki picked the child up in her arms, patting her back and soothing her with soft words.

"I didn't mean—" Julian began in exasperation.

"Shush! You're frightening her," Nikki said softly. She continued to soothe the child until she quieted. Julian was utterly still. His eyes snagged on a fading bruise on the side of the little girl's face. An angry flush suffused his face as he realized why all these children were here.

"Yes," Nikki said softly when she saw his expression. "I'll never be able to understand how a parent, how anyone . . ."

"Nikki! Am I ever glad to see you!" A tall, squarely built woman came hurrying down the hall. She grasped Nikki's hand with an air of desperation. "You can't know how glad I was to get your call. Marla, the cook, smelled gas this morning when she got in! We opened the windows and shut off the gas in back of the stove and it's not leaking anymore, but the children had to settle for cold cereal for breakfast. I've called every plumber in town, and those that aren't off fishing or something won't come until Monday. Just imagine! They don't consider forty-eight kids an emergency! If the kids don't get their lunch pretty soon, we're likely to have a riot."

"Don't worry, Edna. The cavalry has arrived." Noting the older woman's jacket and purse, she asked, "Where were you off to?"

"Oh—the supermarket. To get more peanut butter. I didn't realize we were so dependent on that darn stove."

"Maybe I can help," said Julian. The woman turned her attention to him for the first time and studied him with eyes the color of faded denim.

"Edna Riley, Julian Archer." Nikki introduced the two. "He might be able to help, Edna. He's pretty good with his hands." She only realized the possible double meaning of her statement when she caught Julian's amused glance. A blush crept up her neck to her cheeks.

Edna looked from Nikki to Julian and back again. Her round face lit with a satisfied smile. " 'Bout time," she said. Looking at Julian, she admitted, "I haven't any idea where the leak is. I don't know a thing about plumbing, but if you think you can do something—well, have at it." She nodded them down the hall. "Kitchen's that way, young man. Nikki, you can show him. I'll be back in a bit, and then we can get the kids fed. Tools are in the shed out back, Mr. Archer. Hope we have what you need."

Edna turned her attention to several boys milling at the top of the stairs, who'd turned good-as-gold the instant she'd appeared. "Gino, Tom, Hank, Melvin, and you others—I'll see you when I get back. Just cause Babs is trying to help out in the kitchen doesn't mean that you can break your necks on that banister rail. No MTV tonight"—there was a chorus of boos— "and none for the next week, if there's one more slide. Playground's out back. Now *get.*" With that she stomped away.

Nikki led the way to the kitchen. After a cursory examination of the commercial sized range, Julian left to gather the tools he'd need. He returned to find Nikki sitting in a chair in the kitchen surrounded by children. She seemed so open. Unreserved. She paid each child a special bit of attention. *She opens up so easily to them,* he thought, and felt a little twinge of jealousy. With him, there was still so much of herself she held in reserve.

He asked Nikki to take the children out of the kitchen so that he could turn the gas on for a moment. He checked the pipes with a soapy water solution. Bubbles pinpointed the leak at the connection. It was easily fixed with the roll of Teflon tape and a pipe wrench he found in the tool shed.

"One plumbing bill saved," he told Nikki when she returned to check on his progress. "Not exactly a Prince Charming rescue, but . . ."

"More like the Lone Wrencher from where I stand," she said dryly.

She was pinned by those startling gray eyes. "And you had the nerve to imply that *I* make bad puns!"

Julian barely escaped a swat with a dish towel Nikki was carrying. He dodged around the work table and escaped out the back door. The children who'd trailed in behind Nikki laughed.

When Edna returned, Nikki organized several of the kids into a peanut butter and jelly assembly line to help

the cook and her assistant. The purpose of this enter-
prise appeared to be to get as much peanut butter as
possible on the work table, the kids, and any nearby
grown-ups, while adding grape jelly for color.

Julian saw Edna Riley pull a package of cigarettes
from her pocket and slip out a side door. He followed.
He found her leaning against a corner of the white
painted brick, her lined face tilted up to the sun, eyes
closed. A green cabbage butterfly fluttered near her
head, then crossed the thin stream of smoke rising from
her cigarette and winged away as if offended.

"May I have one of those?" he asked as he approached.

"Sure."

He selected one and accepted a light. He found the
menthol taste of Edna's brand something quite different
from what he was used to, and not altogether pleasant.
"Thanks." He studied the tall, capable-looking woman.
"Calming your nerves?"

Edna chuckled. "Not really. Just a darn bad habit.
By the way, thanks for the stove. I can handle most
things, but plumbing and broken machines throw me."

Julian exhaled a cloud of smoke, his gaze sweeping
over the large play area. There were old tires lashed
together in the shape of a mound, which invited little
hands to climb and explore. There were sandboxes.
Brightly painted animals mounted on coiled springs, for
riding. Swings hung from oak limbs, along with knotted
climb-ropes. He could see Nikki's fine hand at work
on the wooden fence surrounding the play area, where
pink elephants and purple hippopotami paraded beside
other fanciful circus animals.

"Who runs this place, Edna?" he asked.

"Now that depends. Ain't no state or government
thing. Nothing like that, if that's what you mean—

though the university does give us help with counseling for these kids through their graduate program. There's a girl who comes in part-time and types any letters that need to be sent and posts the bills. There's Babs on weekends to watch the kids, and three others take shifts during the week. There's Marla and her helper, another girl who cleans—though the kids have a lot of the responsibility for their own rooms. Several of the kids are out today with people from our special Big Brother and Big Sister Friends. Others are out with Foster Grandparents—that's one of the things which works best." She chuckled again. "The kids call me the Head Dragon in Charge, if that's what you're asking."

Edna took a last drag of her cigarette before crushing it out with her heel. She gave him a measuring look, the sun crinkling the corners of her sharp blue eyes. "Now, if you're really asking where Nikki fits into all this, I think you should just ask her, although a sharp-looking young guy like yourself has probably already figured that out. You be good to that child, now." With that admonition, she moved past him toward the back door.

Julian crushed out his own cigarette and hurried past her as Nikki emerged, struggling with a large cooler. He relieved her of it and set it down on a nearby picnic table as she directed.

"We decided to eat *al fresco*," she explained. "To make up for the uninspired menu."

Marla started filling paper cups and passing them into eager hands. Julian placed an arm around Nikki's slender shoulders and they wandered away. They stopped beneath an ancient magnolia near the fence. The trunk was large. About three feet up the trunk on the back TOMMY + NIC was carved into the smooth gray bark.

"Looks like I have competition," said Julian.

Nikki smiled. "I had forgotten about that. Tommy O'Herlihy lived a few blocks over. He was seven and I was eight and he used to sneak in here through a loose board in the fence, and we would play. Then one day he kissed me on the cheek and told me that I was his girlfriend. I said 'okay' because I liked his freckles and I didn't want him to stop coming to play. It took him almost two afternoons to get that much cut into the tree with the broken pocketknife his dad had given him. Then the gardener told Aunt Rosalie and the fence was repaired. Tommy never came back to finish my name."

"He could have come through the front gate," said Julian.

Nikki shook her head. "No, he couldn't. Aunt Rosalie was something of an eccentric. Very reclusive. She craved privacy. And even had she been different, she was much too conscious of the family position in the old Creole aristocracy to have welcomed a poor Irish kid."

"How long did you live here?" Julian asked her, following as she moved on toward a huge live oak.

"My father left when I was two," Nikki said, her voice betraying no emotion about that event. "Aunt Rosalie—my great-aunt, actually, on the Duval side—brought me here when I was six, after my mother's death." Nikki ran her fingers lightly over the rough black bale, with its flat patches of spreading green moss and silver lichens. Julian had the strange impression that she was saying hello to an old, familiar friend. She went on thoughtfully, "It must have been very difficult for Aunt Rosalie, with her private nature, to make that commitment to bring me up." There was a short pause. "I think that she did love me, in her own way."

A blue jay's scolding from the limb overhead caught Nikki's attention. She didn't see Julian's sharp glance.

She smiled as the jay hopped from limb to limb, still angrily delivering his raucous scold. She turned to lean against the trunk. Her smile encompassed Julian. "I used to spend hours out here everyday with my drawing pads, sketching the trees, the dragonflies, the roses—there used to be a great many of those, but they aren't ideal shrubs for playground use. I'd draw the gardener as he worked; the maid, the cook, the people on the street I saw through the cracks in the fence. Then, when I ran out of new things to draw, I'd make up pictures. The dragonflies turned into fairies. The trees into magical forests. The roses into rosy-cheeked children—why are you looking at me like that?"

"I was thinking about magical forests." Julian's hands slipped up Nikki's bare arms to the shoulders of her sun dress. He pulled her against his deep chest, his wide shoulders sheltering her against a rising March wind. "There are all forms of child abuse, aren't there, Nikki?" Julian murmured.

She stiffened in his arms. "I don't know what you mean?"

"Yes, you do. Are you going to tell me that you were never lonely? Or neglected? Isn't that why you turned this place into a children's shelter after your aunt's death?"

Nikki pushed against his chest, but he refused to release her, as if he knew that she was really pushing against the truth of what he said, hating it. Then two wild Indians rounded the tree and blasted them with imaginary pistols.

"Julian! Let go of me! The kids!" Nikki hissed.

"Seeing people who care for each other won't harm those kids." His gaze caught hers.

His mouth descended toward hers, slowly. Nikki's

heart skipped a beat, then beat double time trying to make up for it as she waited for his lips to find hers.

"Oh, no! Mushy stuff!" cried a girl with dark little pigtails and great, china-blue eyes. *"Ick!"*

Julian's lips stopped their descent only millimeters from Nikki's, a smile twitching up the corners of his mustache. "You betcha, shortcakes. Now, *scat!"*

The order had the immediate effect of drawing every little person within hearing.

"Let go of me!" Nikki insisted again as whistles, whoops, and various bits of advice came from their very-interested audience, which ranged in age from four to fourteen.

"Not yet." Julian's lips were so near that his mustache brushed her mouth as he spoke and she tasted the faint spice of menthol on his breath. Then his mouth claimed hers, warmth erupted at her very core and spread outward. Excitement rushed from her diaphragm up to her throat, and at the same time, downward from where his tongue mastered her mouth.. It was the sound of giggles and applause which drew her back to where she was.

With difficulty, Nikki forced her lips from the aggression of his. "Julian!"

Why did this man always threaten her self-control? He was making her feel under siege. And what in hell gave him the right to look at her like he was now? Like *he* was disappointed in *her* for getting angry? It wasn't as if it weren't only a matter of time before he lost interest.

"Sorry," he said, and released her to a minor chorus of boos, though most of the kids had already drifted away.

By the time Julian and Nikki said good-bye to everyone, the cook and her helper had begun preparing for the evening meal.

NINE

The taxi pulled to a stop at the corner of Canal Street and Rue Chartres. Julian paid the driver and got out, reaching back to assist Nikki.

"Where to now?" she asked as they began walking up Canal street.

"I was thinking of Jackson Square. As I remember, it's a circus on Saturday afternoons."

Nikki laughed. "In that case, we'd better go the other direction."

Nikki guided him on a walking tour of the *Vieux Carre,* down streets that had been laid out deliberately narrow centuries before for the cooling effect of the shade cast by the buildings.

"Most of the *Vieux Carre,* or Old Square, hasn't changed greatly since Andrew Jackson defended the city against the British in 1814," Nikki read, in her best tour-guide voice, from the little book she'd bought for Julian. "Shady balconies framed by lacy iron grill-work—the product of the blacksmiths' forges and hammers of countless slaves—still overlook the streets. Discreet archways lead to quiet inner courtyards, once the heart of these Creole homes.'' As they wandered, occasionally stopping to explore little shops, Nikki recited a capsule history of places of interest, such as Maspero's Exchange, a coffeehouse where the infamous Lafitte brothers carried on much of their business and where, it was said, that they offered the services of their pirate ships to General Andrew Jackson for the defense of New Orleans against the British.

Nikki and Julian crossed Rue St. Louis and passed in front of *"Napoleon's House,"* the house Mayor Girod offered as a sanctuary for the Emperor Napoleon upon his escape from the Island of St. Helena—an escape that never came about.

''I feel like a tourist,'' Nikki admitted as her gaze traveled over the wrought iron balconies of the Pontalba Apartments, which flanked Jackson Square. ''It's all the same, but it doesn't seem like my city anymore.''

Julian's strong arm around her shoulders pulled her near. His warmth felt good against the chill of the wind. Her arm found his waist and she snuggled closer, experiencing the joy that simply being with this man brought her. It was okay to enjoy his company. She just couldn't let it become necessary for him to always be near.

''Did you come here often when you were growing up?'' Julian asked as they made their way through the throngs of people. There was a great deal of activity going on around the art displays arranged against the wrought-iron fence, which surrounded the inner square.

''Oh, yes. Every Saturday,'' she answered with a smile. ''That was my spot.'' She pointed to where an overhanging limb from one of the live oaks in the inner square shaded the sidewalk. ''I would bring a couple of paintings with me—just for color. But I came here to sketch the people. My friend Harold put up his table next to me. He sold cut-out silhouettes. He had a real talent for it. Next to him, Andrea had her worktable. She made little glass sculptures.'' Nikki paused, her eyes widening. ''That fellow over there *is* Harold! He's grown a beard, but it's him. And there's Andrea! Oh, Julian, I can't believe they're still here,'' she cried joyfully. ''It's been so long since I saw them.''

''Do I have reason to be jealous?'' Julian frowned savagely as Nikki dragged him forward.

''Are you?''

''Absolutely.''

''Good.''

Julian had only been teasing, but his fist clenched at his side as Nikki ran up to a gangly young man in patched jeans, who caught her up in an embrace and kissed her enthusiastically. A slender, black-haired girl pried the two apart, so that she, too, could hug Nikki. Obviously another of Nikki's old friends.

It wasn't until Nikki introduced the pair to him as Harold Williams and his wife Andrea that Julian relaxed completely. He even managed to smile and extend his hand. Harold clasped it firmly.

''So, did you get Nikki out of that job that she'd locked herself into, and back here for good? Or is this just a visit?'' Harold asked later as Andrea led Nikki away to say hello to some other old friends on the other side of the square.

''Just playing tourist,'' Julian replied. Inspecting some samples of Harold's work, he added, ''These are good.''

''Thanks. I like what I do.'' Harold picked up a pair of scissors and a piece of black construction paper and began cutting what appeared to be a formal pattern. ''I'm not in the same class as Nicole, though, I know that. If I'd had a third of her talent . . . She was the fastest pencil on the square. And easily the best. What she could see in people, and then put on paper or canvas, it's almost as if she had some mystical inner vision. Something not quite of this world. Something artists like Picasso and Turner had, each in their own way."

Harold moved away to show some of his work to an older couple with New Jersey accents. Deftly he made two sales, cutting out profiles of each as they waited. After they had gone, Julian asked, "I get the impression that you know her well."

"Oh, yeah. Since Andrea and I came down from Natchez, and started working the square. Then Nikki went away to college and married that jerk of a football player. He seemed to put the *gris-gris* on everything for her. Did you know that she had the chance to study at one of the best schools in Paris? Then she got blocked. We haven't seen her in a couple of years." Harold completed his silhouette. It turned out to be a Scotty dog. It looked full of life, for a mere shadow.

"Harold," Julian asked, "why do you think Nikki stopped painting?"

"I'm not a shrink," Harold said.

"You're an artist."

He shrugged his thin, flannel plaid shoulder and looked thoughtful. "I really don't know. If I had to guess, well, can you imagine the kind of sensitivity it took to produce what Nikki could? To have that kind of sensitivity in an insensitive world must be an invitation to pain. Her aunt died—and the old lady was always laying the biggest guilt trip on her you ever saw. Then, she got involved with that barbarian—I met him once. After that, maybe, she went into overload. Her receptors just shut down in self-defense. It's a shame. Nikki's a great kid. Nothing like the rest of the family."

"What do you mean?"

"Maybe you don't know them—*the* Duvals? As in New Orleans bankers for umpteen generations? Very *'Old South.'* I swear, if her aunt had known that Nikki would take most of her inheritance and start that children's shelter, the old lady would have refused to die."

Harold looked at Julian as one man to another, his gaze astute. "Maybe now that she's started to open up again in other areas of her life, she'll get her art back."

A few minutes later, Nikki and Harold's slim, dark-haired wife rejoined them. Julian put his arm around Nikki's shoulders as Harold and Andrea showed their wares to browsers. Making a sale seemed to be as much a matter of showmanship as talent. Julian studied Nikki's face in profile as she watched her friends. Her violet eyes were shadowed beneath the curl of her lashes. The day had helped him understand some of the mysteries behind them, but there were still more, some he'd probably never fathom.

"I didn't know that you paid the bills at Duval House, too," Julian said.

Nikki turned and looked up at him, studying the strong planes and angles in his face, framed by his dark, wind-whipped hair. There was a softness in his gray eyes that wasn't characteristic. She was used to seeing dark passion, or silver anger, or that stark, penetrating gaze that saw through people or problems. This soft light made her heart swell and ache all at the same time.

"I don't really. The money is invested in municipal bonds and a lot of other investments. The dividends fund the home. There's a board of trustees, on which I have a seat.''

Andrea sold two pirate ships and a doe and fawn on spindly legs. "That's it for me," she announced as the group wandered away. The rising wind was beginning to buffet her fragile treasures. Nikki helped as Andrea began wrapping the pieces in tissue and nesting them in a large box. As Julian watched her graceful movements, what Harold said about her starting to re-open her life came back to him.

"Harold," Julian asked impulsively, "is there an art-supply store nearby, or anywhere I could buy a sketchbook?"

"For Nikki? Sure thing."

He delved into a pasteboard box beside his lounge chair and came out with a thick pad and a package of thick leaded pencils with peel-away barrels.

"You'll need those," Julian protested.

"Naw. I'm ready to pack it in for the day, too, before this wind tears everything apart. I only bring this in case I get an idea that I want to record to work on later. There's nothing in the book. Take it."

He refused any money. Julian took it and thanked him.

"Nikki."

She turned. Her smile died on her lips as she saw what Julian held out to her. He put the drawing pad and pencils into her hands and she looked down at them dumbly for a moment. Angling shafts of sunlight pierced the wind-tossed limbs overhead, dappling her mahogany hair with spots of moving sunlight. He tenderly smoothed a wind-whipped strand away from her cheek, tucking it behind her ear, only to have it whip right back.

"No, Julian. You don't understand," Nikki began as

she looked up into his face. She saw the almost harsh angles of his face, his hair alive in the wind, the shine in his eyes as he gazed at her, and a special excitement began to build within her. She closed her eyes, almost in fear.

"I know that I don't understand," Julian told her softly. "But I think the woman in my bed last night had stopped running away from herself." He touched the sketchbook in her hands. "This is a part of you, Nikki." He lifted her chin and forced her to look at him. "You have to try." Nikki's eyes widened. He thought she was going to deny what he'd told her. Instead, still clutching the sketchbook, she turned and ran into the crowd.

Julian started to follow Nikki, then thought better of it. He watched her disappear through the gate into the park.

When he found her in the park half an hour later, she was sitting under a huge oak tree. Her head was bent over the sketchpad and the hand holding the pencil flew over the page. He waited at a distance, not wanting to disturb her.

The park within the wrought-iron fence was an island of peace amid the frenzy of the square. A bandstand had been erected near one fence, and several musicians were setting up. There were a few couples scattered about on the grass, and on one bench a man dozed with a newspaper over his face. Near the central statue of Andrew Jackson was an old man with a strange looking cart. Pigeons by the hundreds were congregated on the walks and grass around him. Several small children stood near his cart, with pigeons on their heads and outstretched arms. Their delighted giggles drifted to Julian on the breeze.

Nikki had put the pencil down and was gazing out

over the park. Julian crossed the grass to where she sat. As he stooped down, he noticed that her eyes were shiny with unshed tears. "Nikki, is something wrong?" he asked anxiously. "I hope I . . ." He trailed off, suddenly unsure of what to say. Giving her that sketch pad had been the wrong thing, he thought. It was too much pressure for her to handle, as if he expected her to be able to draw on command.

Nikki's face showed a kind of confusion that increased his concern. But when she looked up at him, she smiled. "There's nothing wrong, Julian. Nothing at all. I just realized that I've been drawing. I sat here with the blank paper in front of me like a rebuke. All that empty whiteness to fill." She paused a moment to take a deep breath. "Then I started watching the pigeon man." She waved a hand toward the old, raggedly-dressed gentleman in the center of the square. "There was a little girl with him. She looked to be four or five. Sandy hair and freckles. Cute as a button. And the old guy had given her a handful of birdseed. That's what he does," she said, explaining the cart. "He has a tub of birdseed in that cart he wheels around, and a bank to take donations. Nobody seems to know where he came from, but the birds love him and his customers. Anyway, he gave the little girl some seed, and she was holding it out to the pigeons. The expression on her face was—well . . ." She trailed off. "Here." She handed him the sketchbook.

A drawing had been penciled on the page. It showed the outline of the statue and the flower bed around it. The pigeon man stood by his cart, his eyes fixed on some distant point, a weary kind of patience etched into his features. The little girl's face was raised as if she were trying to catch a glimpse of the pigeon perched on her curly head. A look somewhere between wonder and consternation was on her face. She was biting one side of her lip, and her pudgy fingers were curled around the feet of a bird that was clutching one tiny thumb. "I didn't even realize I was drawing it." Nikki's voice was wistful.

He lifted her to her feet and pulled her to him. His voice thick with emotion, he said, "I knew you could, Nikki. It was there in you all the time."

The sad, sweet sound of a trumpet filtered through the hushed conversation at nearby tables. Nikki leaned back in her chair at one of the patio tables in the Cafe du Monde. She held the half-empty cup of chicory-laced coffee between the palms of her hands. The heat from the brew felt good. The evening had gotten a little chilly, and she shivered slightly as the cool night breeze brushed her bare shoulders.

Midnight had come too soon. The evening had been glorious. She and Julian had gone to three nightclubs, listened to some of the best jazz in the city. During the evening she had wondered how it was she could feel so in touch with this man. It was like meeting someone you had known in another life. The pull was tremendous. And it was dangerous.

The day had been a series of awakenings, she thought. Julian had given her back pieces of herself that she'd thought were lost forever. Especially her art. It was almost like being blind and then suddenly being able to see again through some miracle. She looked thoughtfully at the sketch of the little girl with the pigeon man. She could see it. Her sketches had a life to them—the thing they had been lacking since Bob's death. But would it last? She couldn't bear the thought of losing it all again.

"Nikki . . . a penny?"

Nikki looked up at the man who was sitting across the table from her. His eyes were so dark tonight, she thought abstractly. "I was just thinking about today. It's been a very special day, Julian."

"Yes. It has."

The low timbre of Julian's voice raised a chill along her spine. She shivered. "Are you cold?" Julian moved his chair around the table until it was next to hers. "That sundress doesn't keep you very warm. Here. I guess I should give this to you now." He reached under the table to get the package he had been carrying with him since their exploration of the shops in the Quarter. With a teasing smile, he opened the bag and drew something out.

Before Nikki was the most beautiful shawl she had ever seen. It was woven of a soft, smoky rose thread. A design of rampant foliage and flowers ran long each edge. The flowers seemed to strain toward the center, where a full moon was depicted. The colors were muted, as though they were observed in the light of that soft moon.

Nikki marveled at the workmanship and artistry of the garment. Her questing hand smoothed the silkiness of the fine fabric. A cheaper shawl would have had the design printed on it, but this was woven in. In the soft light of the cafe Nikki could just make out the subtlety of hue that shadowed the "man in the moon" face, the shading of the flowers and leaves. It was an extraordinary work of art.

Nikki raised shiny eyes to Julian's face. His smile was warm. "It is beautiful, isn't it?" he said. "I knew you would love it the minute I saw it." Shaking out the shawl so that the ten-inch fringe fell straight, he draped it around her shoulders. The warmth of it cradled her.

"You're beautiful," Julian said softly. "I'm going to enjoy buying lovely things for you."

There it was again, that assumption of ownership, that they would be together. What about *her* life? Did he think she would just give up all she had worked for these last five years for some temporary fling with him? Where would she be when he got tired of her?

"How about a stroll along the Moon Walk?" Julian asked.

The turbulence of the weather matched Nikki's mood. The wind whipped her hair into her eyes as they made their way to the stairs over the seawall. Julian's arm around her shoulders steadied her as they topped the wall. Farther on, the board walkway stretched along the top of a low levee. The level of the river was high, Nikki thought. Spring melt-off must be heavy this year. There was a bricked stair that led right down to the water in front of the boardwalk. The quickly glimpsed moonlight gilded the rough wavelets that lapped at the bricks. As they crossed the boardwalk to find an unoccupied bench, the trumpet player at the other end of it started another tune—something low and bluesy. Nikki settled onto a bench, tucking her feet under her. Julian sat beside her. With a warm hand, he touched her cheek and guided her head against his shoulder. The muscles moved beneath her cheek as he slid an arm around her shoulders. She could just barely make out the beat of his pulse where her face touched his chest.

"This is beautiful," he said. "All the times I've been to New Orleans, I've never taken the time to enjoy it. And I can see why this is a favorite spot for lovers." He nodded toward a young couple who were seated on the bricks facing the water. The young man's arms were circled protectively around the girl. The young man moved his head to the side and whispered something in the girl's ear. Their soft laughter floated to Nikki on the wind. She looked away when they kissed, embarrassed to be eavesdropping on their love.

Nikki fought an urge to nestle closer under Julian's sheltering arm. She needed this too much—this closeness. A gust of wind took her breath away, lashing at her hair. "Looks like rain. Maybe we should get back to the hotel," Julian suggested.

"No!" Her voice was sharp as she pulled away from him and stood up. "I mean, not right now." She walked toward the horn player, whose case was laid open before him to collect donations. Her eyes were in shadow from the street lamps that lined the walk. They took in the wind-tossed water, the silhouette of the musician, the gleam of the brass horn in the dim light. The music was counterpoint to the picture, and her mood.

The hotel. Another night with Julian. And another. And another. The prospect was beautiful. But the conclusion? He would gradually lose interest, and he would leave her drained and empty and aching. She'd been a fool to think she could have a relationship with him. She just wasn't capable of playing those sort of adult games.

"Nikki. Let's go back. You're tired and it's been a long day." Julian placed that protective arm around her shoulders again. "Tomorrow we'll leave for Houston. There's a room in the penthouse that would be a perfect studio for you to paint in. I want you to see it."

Nikki whipped around to face him, roughly pulling herself free of his grasp. A strange panic washed over her, and she trembled. Go back to Houston! A room to paint! What about Monday morning? What about her job? What about her apartment? Just leave it all behind? That was what he expected.

"And what makes you think I'm going back to Houston with you?" Her hands clenched spasmodically in the fabric of her shawl. "It's been a lovely weekend, Julian, but I have a job. A home. Responsibilities. I can't just leave them."

Julian was suddenly very still. He was looking at her with a strangely calm expression on his face. But his eyes blazed. Nikki expected the voice that came from his throat to be forceful enough to overpower the growing wail of the wind and the sound of thunder in the distance. Instead, she had to strain to hear him. "Nicole, I'm asking you to come back to Houston with me. To be with me."

Voices railed in Nikki's head. She was losing herself to him. She was too dependent on him, already. She needed love, commitment. What would she be when he left? And he *would* leave. She had needed Bob, and he had stifled her. And, then, when he had died, she had been unable to draw, to paint. Julian had given her hope that she could paint again—but what if he left? She would be alone. No job. No family. No—life. She couldn't risk that. She had a life now. She wouldn't throw it all away for a few months—or weeks—with this man.

The wind beat at Nikki, slapping her hair against her cheeks. She stared at Julian. He was so strong. His eyes burned into hers, his will pulled at her. She had to get away.

Nikki turned toward the stairway. She brushed roughly past the trumpeter who was closing his horn case. As she reached the top of the seawall, the first stinging drops of rain pelted her and the wind tore the shawl from her hands. She raced down the steps. Everywhere people were running for shelter. Nikki didn't see them.

Some rationality came back to her when she reached the street at the Square. She looked back. She could just barely make out a silhouette. Julian stood atop the seawall. The wind tugged at something in his hand. Her shawl.

The rain began in earnest as Nikki turned to run for a distant taxi.

The door of the suite sitting room slammed against the wall. Julian strode inside, his eyes sweeping the empty room.

"Nikki!" He wasn't surprised when there was no answer. The anger that had fueled him during the hurried walk to the hotel suddenly fled as he sensed the absence of any other human presence. Of her presence.

Julian shook his head violently, flinging rain water from his soaking hair. It spattered the flocked wallpaper behind him. He stalked through the open door of her room.

The closet stood open and empty. The drawers in the ornate French Provincial dresser also stood open, as though she had packed too hurriedly to take the time to close them. Julian stooped to retrieve a delicate hammered-gold earring from where it lay forgotten on the carpet, and remember how it had looked against her skin—was it only last night?

He walked into the bathroom and pulled a fresh towel from its perch in the chrome rack near the basin. He stripped the soaked shirt from his body, dropping it carelessly on the floor. As he dried his face and hair, he saw that there was nothing left to bear witness to the love they had shared there that morning. Throwing the towel down with an oath, he stalked from the bathroom.

He was halfway through the bedroom when a bitter

glance at the bed where they had spent the night revealed a corner of the sketchbook underneath.

Julian sat heavily on the edge of the mattress. Pulling the pad out, he opened it to the drawing of the pigeon man and the little freckle-faced girl. She had captured in the old man the eyes of age; the child was alight with discovery in a world that was good and new.

He turned the page. And held very still. The face that looked back at him was strongly chiselled. There was cynicism. Humor. Strength. And in the sharp eyes, he found a certain vulnerability, a softening compassion. The sketch was of himself. This was how he looked when he looked at Nikki.

This was how he looked in love.

Julian went back into the sitting room, closing the door on Nikki's empty room. He splashed bourbon into a glass and lifted it with a hand that trembled. A trace of Nikki's perfume still hung in the air, softly maddening.

The raw liquor burned its way to his stomach. His gut twisted with the pain he felt. He hurt. And he hurt for her. The needy eyes of that little girl in the Mardi Gras painting came back to him, and his glass rattled against the glass topped bar as he set it down. There was moisture on his cheeks that wasn't rain.

Love. The word ripped into him. He did love.

For the first time he understood the pain which had made her withdraw. She'd been a bright and sensitive child, neglected. Always aching for love from people incapable of giving. As a young woman she had tried to give the best of herself to someone—then everything had gone wrong.

Oh, Nicole! He longed to pull her to him and give her everything of himself. But he couldn't force her to love him. And now, he understood the risk that she was unwilling to take. He loved. He hurt.

Nikki couldn't bear to be that vulnerable again.

And nothing he could do would change that.

TEN

Nikki became aware of voices raised somewhere in anger. It seemed a great distance away. The sleeping pill she'd taken the evening before hadn't worked, so she'd given up and taken another one around 3:00 a.m. Then, at last, she'd been pulled into sleep, like being sucked into deep waters. Now she was paying the price. Her tongue felt thick and cottony, her eyelids grainy and hard to hold open. She struggled to stay atop the deep pool, to maintain awareness. It was important. There were things she had to say.

Then she remembered that everything had been said and gave up. She pulled the blanket over her head and squirmed into a less uncomfortable position on the hard sofa in Edna's office, where she'd made her bed. Soon, she was being pulled back under.

The blanket was rudely flipped away, leaving Nikki to huddle into the warmth of the oversized pajamas Edna had lent her.

"Good morning."

Never had two words carried such sarcastic inflection. Nikki opened her eyes. She somehow wasn't surprised to see a dark, strongly shaped face with deepset, penetrating gray eyes bent over her. Her lids were drawn irresistibly closed.

Julian shook her shoulder. "Wake up, Nicole. I want to talk to you." His tone was dry. Impersonal. He might have been giving the stock exchange report.

She shook her head slightly, eyes still firmly closed.

" 'M awake," she got out past an uncooperative tongue. "Just groggy. Pills haven't worn off."

She sensed Julian moving away. Heard a rattle, which she identified as capsules in a plastic Rx bottle, her prescription, which she'd left on Edna's desk.

"These?" he asked.

She nodded without looking.

"How many did you take?" he demanded. For the first time there was some emotion in his deep voice.

Nikki held up two fingers.

There was a sharp "twang" as the bottle of sleeping pills hit the bottom of an empty metal wastebasket. "I won't have you abusing these! They're not candy, Nicole!" he told her harshly.

"Doctor said 'twas okay. They're mild," she murmured. After listening a few seconds more for anything further he might say, and hearing nothing but his footsteps retreating, Nikki slipped back into oblivion.

Her next touch with reality was as someone sat her up and tucked the blanket around her. A mug of strong black coffee was placed in her hands and steadied. After a few sips, Nikki discovered that it was no longer completely impossible to open her eyes. A few more sips, and she could hold them open without too much difficulty.

It might have been better not to. Julian sat across from her on the edge of Edna's desk. The sleeves of his heavy, cable knit sweater were pushed back, past the tautly muscled forearms crossed over his chest. His face was impassive. His gray eyes, shadowed by thick lashes, watched her intently. They told her nothing of the thoughts going on behind them. The only clue to his anger were the tightly bunched muscles at his jaw.

"Julian?"

"You're awake enough to talk. Good."

Nikki sighed, feeling all too awake. "We said everything last night."

"We said *nothing*!" His gray eyes pinned her beneath the lash of his anger. He rose abruptly and strode to the window, opening the shutters to the early morning sun. "I'm sorry," he said at length, his voice so soft, she could barely hear it. "I didn't come here to argue, but to talk. What is it, Nikki? What's so terrible about asking you to come back to Houston with me? Can you tell me that you don't enjoy what we have together?"

Nikki looked at his squared shoulders, the set of his dark head, and was sorry that she'd injured his pride. She shouldn't have been so abrupt, she realized. But he'd made her feel so damned vulnerable, she'd had to get away before she broke down in tears. "I never meant that I didn't want to see you again, although it might be best that way. I have a life in Abbeville. A job. People who depend on me. I can't drop all the other facets of my life and go running off with you."

"You'd have your painting." He turned back to face her.

"I don't know that!" she cried. Didn't he understand that she couldn't give up everything that she had built when there were no guarantees that she'd ever be able to do serious work again? Alone with Julian in a strange city, with nothing of her own to strive for, she would grow clinging and demanding. What was destined, at best, to be a short-lived relationship would end with her heart in a million fragments. He was already too important to her. She had to get out while she could!

Nikki pushed her thick hair away from her face and struggled to explain in a way that would ease his wounded pride. Men like Julian Archer were used to being the ones to make the breaks. "I'm going back to Abbeville, Julian, because that's where my life is."

"No, it isn't. You're just pretending at life!"

"There are people depending on me." She straightened, stung.

Julian pushed his fists deep into the pockets of his cords and moved to stand before her. "Cut to the heart of it, Nikki. The bottom line."

She dropped her eyes. "I . . . don't want to go with you." There was a moment of utter stillness in which she couldn't meet his eyes. She heard his harsh expulsion of breath.

What had he expected her to say? he thought bitterly. That she loved him and couldn't think of a life without him? "All right. If that's the way you want it," he said, his voice a rasp.

Something within her leapt in pain at his easy acquiescence. If he had loved her, wouldn't he have told her? Argued with her? If he felt what she needed him to feel for her, would he have ever let her go?

Julian resumed his seat on the edge of Edna's desk. His features were coldly chiseled. The expression in his eyes was all cold anger. "That's your choice," he said evenly. "But it occurs to me that we have some unfinished business to take care of."

Nikki, who'd been studying the bottom of her coffee mug in misery, looked up, struggling to make sense of the abrupt change of direction. "What do you mean? What business?"

"You still owe me a painting. I kept my side of the bargain, and didn't pursue an investigation into Colomb's dealings with Grimes. There may even have been some criminal charges—conspiracy to defraud comes to mind—leveled against Colomb."

Nikki gasped at this sudden stranger. Rising anger helped her find her tongue. "That horse has been dead for a long time! You know that Colomb wasn't involved with Grimes's embezzlement schemes."

Julian's mustache curved upward at one corner in a smile that chilled her. "I don't know whether to applaud your loyalty, or laugh at your naïveté. Yes, Colomb was involved. No, I don't believe that you were party to it. I have faith in your personal integrity. But someone conspired with Grimes. As I examined the records you gave me, I discovered things like work orders for roustabout crews which had been initialed by a certain gang-pusher—according to your own records—several months after the man had left Colomb.

"Then, there's the matter of the dock space, which Archer Oil had been leasing from Colomb in Intracoastal City. There's no record of payment for this in your company records because payments have been made to your father-in-law. According to Archer's records, the first several of these checks were cashed. I would guess that the money was paid directly to Grimes. Later, the checks were endorsed directly over to Grimes. The audacity of it amazes me!"

Nikki's cold fingers circled her coffee mug, her eyes on the dark liquid within as she examined his words and tasted the truth in them. She felt betrayed. A feeling of nausea rose in her throat. Colomb didn't deserve to keep the contract. Still, there were more people to be considered than just Pop Colomb.

"I gave you a painting," she whispered raggedly.

"I paid you for that," he reminded her.

"I didn't ask for money!"

"You cashed the check."

"I signed it over to Duval House, to start a scholarship fund. You can take it off your taxes."

Julian's eyes narrowed. "Okay. You gave me a painting," he conceded with the generosity of a man certain of ultimate victory. He rose and went to the other side of the desk and flipped through the address book lying on its polished surface. He pulled the speaker phone to him and tapped out a number. Nikki could hear ringing at the other end of the line.

"Hello?"

Nikki labored under another surprise. It was her father-in-law's voice. Her eyes flew back to Julian's impassive face as she tried to understand what he was up to.

"This is Julian Archer, Mr. Colomb. I'd like to talk some business."

"Mr. Archer!" Pop's voice was instantly toadying. "Well, ain't this a nice surprise! I thought you'd be too busy enjoying New Orleans to think about business. I told Nikki to just relax and to show you a real good time."

There was a slight but unmistakable inflection in the man's voice. Nikki thought that she would be ill. Everything was beginning to take on a gray swirl— everything except Julian's eyes. The bright contempt in them was as piercing as a blade.

Surely he didn't think that she . . . ?

"Mr. Archer, you still there?" Pop's voice came back with a thread of worry when Julian didn't immediately reply.

"Still here." His contempt colored his voice. "Colomb, I'll come right to the point. Archer Oil will be running the Indian Point Lease from now on. I want to buy your company. Name a price.''

After only a moment's hesitation, Nikki heard Pop name a six-digit figure. Julian immediately made a counter offer, cutting the amount by two-hundred thousand dollars. The amount wasn't exactly generous, but it was fair. As Pop must have realized because he agreed almost immediately.

"Then it's settled," Julian pronounced. "Have your lawyers draw up a contract and send it to me in care of the Houston Office."

"Yes, sir, Mr. Archer. That I will do. I've been thinking about getting out for awhile now, my health being what it is. And my boy's told me he wants to go to law school."

"Send me those papers," was all Julian said before hanging up.

"Where does this leave the people who work for Colomb?" Nikki asked quietly.

"People like Bergeron and Schexnader? Funny, your father-in-law didn't ask that question." Archer's tone was scathing.

"Just what do you intend to do?"

"They will be absorbed into Archer Oil and continue to do just as they're doing now. I don't believe it would be considered bragging if I say that my company offers one of the best insurance and benefit programs in the country. They may even realize higher pay. Of course, they will be required to take the same proficiency test that all Archer employees take before being placed in such a potentially hazardous area. It's no accident that Archer has the best safety record of any of the major oil companies. Oh . . . I'm afraid the test is written.''

He let the implication sink in.

Nikki felt as if her muscles had been encased in

cement. Only her heart continued to thump, and that most painfully. Who was this man, who sat there looking at her so dispassionately? His features might have been cast of bronze, perfect and cold. "You wouldn't, Julian!" She shook her head, not wanting to believe that he was capable of this.

"Standard procedure."

Nikki still didn't want to believe that he was capable of hurting innocent people. She'd always known that there was a certain ruthlessness about him or he couldn't have accomplished what he had, turning Archer Oil from a successful independent company into a major international corporation. And *he* knew that she had no choice but to do as he wanted. He was only giving her the time to realize it!

"Bastard!" she hissed.

Julian's mouth curved in a wintry smile. "That's not a very original observation of my character," he drawled, moving back to the window. "My ex-wife used it so often, I came to consider it my pet name."

Nikki was surprised into momentarily forgetting her anger. "I didn't know that you'd been married."

Julian gave her a dark look. "There are a great many things about me that you don't know and never cared enough to find out," he told her dryly. "With twenty-twenty hindsight, I can see that the marriage was damned from the start. I went into it for the wrong reasons. Oh, I like Katrina. The sex was good. Katrina's father wanted the wedding to consummate a merger with his shipping company. But Katrina wanted to be the darling of the jet-set crowd. I wanted a family. We had some very fundamental differences."

Nikki put her face in her hands, lost in a sea of conflicting emotions, still too influenced by the effects of the sleeping pills to sort them properly. The one that came to the fore was anger. No matter what disappointments Julian must have suffered in his marriage, this situation had nothing to do with that one. He had no right to threaten the security of innocent people. He wasn't the man she had thought, after all.

"What do you want of me, Julian?" she asked wearily, expecting for him to demand again that she go to Houston and live with him.

"Just what I said," he answered at length. "A painting."

"A painting? You want a painting? And you'll see that none of the Colomb people lose their jobs arbitrarily?"

"No. Not exactly," Julian said slowly. "You lose your job. You can't work for Archer Oil."

"I see. If that's what you want," Nikki agreed. She couldn't keep the sadness from rising within her. She hid it behind closed eyes. "The paintings in Abbeville are all I have. Take what you want."

"I'm sorry," Archer drawled. "I don't seem to have made myself very clear. I don't want any of those. I want you to paint a portrait of my grandmother. We'll leave as soon as you can get your things together. Her house in Bay St. Louis is only an hour's drive from here."

Nikki sat very still. Her eyes, which had flown open, were fixed on his face. His expression gave nothing away. Was this some new game?

"I won't be staying, if that's what you're afraid of," he drawled sardonically. "I'll drop you off and leave."

"And when I finish?"

Archer gave an indifferent shrug. "You're over twenty-one, Nicole. You'll be free to go where you wish and do whatever you want."

ELEVEN

The rented Mercedes pulled through a wrought-iron gate and up a shady circular drive of red brick. Nikki stared at the house long seconds after Julian had shut off the ignition. It wasn't large, she noticed. But the stark whiteness, and the surrounding split-leaf philodendron and other dark green foliage, set off the simplicity of the house's geometric curves and planes. Then Julian was opening her door and helping her out of the car.

"Are you all right?" Julian's voice seemed to come from far away. "Your hands are cold."

Nikki turned to face him, a sardonic smile curving her mouth. Like a surgeon wielding a scalpel, with a few deft strokes this man had cut up and restructured her life. Was she all right? She didn't know, but she was certain that her life would never be the same. Nikki started to move away. Julian moved with her, his strong hand cupping her elbow.

Inside were more of the startlingly white plaster walls and Art Deco lines, set off by the large windows and open airy spaces. A uniformed maid informed Julian that Mrs. Harrington, his grandmother, was on the patio. Julian led Nikki through the house to a small enclosed courtyard of terra cotta tile complete with a miniature fountain where splashing water captured the dappling sunlight.

But by far the brightest thing on the patio was the tall woman who lay aside her newspaper and rose as Julian led Nikki forward. The woman wore a sweeping rainbows-on-scarlet caftan. Her coarse gray hair was cut in a short cap, accentuating her strong-featured face. Wrinkles radiated from the corners of sharp black eyes which flicked over her grandson, then studied Nikki curiously. Nikki returned her stare. After a moment, sharp lines bracketed the woman's mouth as it lifted slightly in a grudgingly respectful smile at Nikki's boldness.

Quite a woman, Nikki thought. Definitely a force to be reckoned with, and one who controls her own destiny.

"Julian, dear. It's good to see you," the older woman said as she leaned forward to accept Julian's kiss on her cheek. Her black eyes went almost immediately back to Nikki.

"Gram, this is Nicole Duval, the . . . uh . . . friend I mentioned to you on the phone this morning." Julian gave his grandmother's hand a subtle squeeze.

"Your friend," his grandmother acknowledged. As Nikki offered her hand, Kate Harrison accepted with aplomb. She allowed a look of comprehension and welcome to settle over her features—just as if Julian *had* mentioned bringing someone with him.

He hadn't. In fact, he had barely said anything at all. He had only asked if she would be free today. His reticence, and something in his tone, had caused her to be concerned. She'd been right. Something was wrong. She'd known that the moment she had seen his face.

Feminine instinct told her she was shaking hands with the cause.

"Mrs. Harrison. A pleasure to meet you," Nikki murmured automatically.

"Nikki is going to paint that portrait that I've been asking you to sit for," Julian said, catching his grandmother's eyes. Kate Harrison's brows rose beneath her fringe of gray bangs. *And I thought I was past any surprises at my age*, she thought. Catching the mocking gleam in her grandson's eyes, she drew herself up as if accepting a challenge and turned back to his protegé with a wide smile.

"How *marvelous*! As I said on the phone, Julian, I'll be very glad to sit for your friend." *Or, should I say with her?* she thought. "Please have a seat. I'll ask Cindy to bring more coffee."

As Julian helped Nikki to be seated at the patio table, his grandmother excused herself. She found her maid and asked her to take down a certain portrait that hung in the dining room and to hide it in an upstairs closet.

Despite the tension that Julian's nearness had caused, Nikki found herself beginning to relax in the pleasant atmosphere. "This is lovely," she said of the small courtyard to Kate Harrison as she rejoined them. Much of the plaster wall surrounding them was heavy with vines of purple wisteria. The wall dipped low to the south between a small building and the main house, offering an excellent view of the mouth of St. Louis Bay and the Mississippi Sound beyond.

"Thank you, dear. It is my favorite place in all the world." Kate swept the scene with loving eyes.

Nikki wondered, as the older woman's eyes lit briefly on her preoccupied grandson, just how much she knew about the relationship between Nikki and Julian. The strain between them had to be obvious, although Mrs.

Harrison was ignoring it with gracious southern charm. "Ah! Here's our coffee," their hostess said as the maid arrived.

Nikki accepted her cup and her attention wandered to the distant scene, leaving Julian and his grandmother to carry the conversation. She was distantly aware of undercurrents in the low voices, but she didn't feel up to trying to sort them out.

She suddenly didn't feel up to much of anything. If Julian would just leave, maybe she could put her jumbled feelings into some sort of perspective. She had to decide what she was going to do. She had agreed to paint the portrait, but afterward?

"You seem tired, Nicole. Would you like me to show you to the guest house? You can freshen up and rest for a bit. There'll be plenty of time for you and I to get acquainted later."

Nikki's eyes found Julian's face. It was as impassive as it had been this morning. "Yes, thank you. I am tired," she agreed, rising.

"I should go." Julian rose, too, earning him a sharp glance from his grandmother.

"Nonsense!" Her look told Julian that she was intent on getting his *friend* settled, so that the two of them could have a private conversation. "You've only just arrived."

"Okay, Gram," Julian conceded, a half-smile twitching his lips. "But I'll show Nikki to the guest house." His face was grim as he turned to Nikki and indicated a gate in the low wall. She brushed by him, wondering why he was prolonging this charade. It was obvious now that the attempted conquest was over, he wanted to be rid of her as quickly as possible.

Julian escorted her down a pleasant sandstone path to the small building she had noticed earlier. The guest house had one bedroom—where she discovered her things had been unpacked—a bath, a tiny kitchenette, and a comfortable living area. Julian led her through the rooms in cool silence, answering her occasional questions with as few words as possible. When they reached the other door he brought her onto a large private deck, which was hidden from the main house and courtyard, and overlooked a private boathouse and dock.

Julian propped his forearms on the bleached redwood railing and studied the waves along the far shore for a few moments. "It's okay if you want to call me a bastard again," he said quietly.

"For manipulating me? It hardly matters."

He stared into her emotionless eyes and cold regret washed over him. He could have taken her anger, but not this indifference. She didn't need to call him a bastard—that's what he'd been calling himself.

"Maybe one day, Nicole, you'll grow up!" His face went dark with frustration.

Nikki gasped as if he'd struck her. "How can I when other people insist on arranging my life?"

The muscles along his jaw line tensed, his eyes narrowed. That she was right only fueled his anger. He took a step nearer, his voice tightly controlled, "Maybe where you're concerned my actions have been controlled by my emotions. Those actions haven't always been right—but at least I'm not afraid to feel!"

Nikki shrank from him, but found the corner of the railing at her back. "I'm not afraid to feel! I'm not afraid—!"

Suddenly, she was in his arms, her mouth under his. He forced her lips open, so that he could invade her warm mouth with his tongue. At first she resisted, her body stiff and unyielding against his. But, as the power of his kiss seeped into her, it became desire instead of anger. She couldn't stop the response that surged through her, softening her muscles, causing her to return the pressure of his mouth. A soft moan escaped from her throat as her fingers slid up the strong column of his neck into the short crisp hair at its nape.

Julian smoothed his hands down her back, molding her more closely to him, then cupping the roundness of her buttocks, pressing her more firmly against his hardness.

"Julian—no! I can't . . ." Nikki gasped, breaking away.

"Oh, God, Nikki." Julian turned his face against the curve of her shoulder. With excruciating effort, she pulled her body away from his. Chest still heaving with reaction, she looked squarely into his smoky gray eyes. "I'm not afraid to feel, Julian. But *feeling* means more than sexual attraction. And sexual attraction isn't enough."

Julian's hands dropped from where they held her waist. His eyebrows came together over his nose as a frown twisted his features. His mouth opened a little, as if he were about to say something, then a stillness settled over him.

Julian straightened, but his eyes never left Nikki's face. In a voice that made a shiver run up her spine, he agreed, "No. You're right. Sexual attraction *isn't* enough." He turned and walked away.

TWELVE

Kate Harrison had been a bit astounded when Nikki had asked to be driven into Bay St. Louis to rent a car. Her eyebrows had disappeared beneath her bangs. Nikki had to explain that the trip to Bay St. Louis had been rather spur-of-the-moment, and that she hadn't come prepared for an extended stay. She could see the wheels turning in the woman's mind when Nikki had assured her that she would be back. She obviously had believed Nikki was making her getaway.

Not that it hadn't crossed Nikki's mind. She'd driven home, packed a couple of bags and her art supplies into her compact, and left Mrs. DesHotels a vague note saying that she'd be gone for awhile. Then, after she returned the rental car, she went to have it out with Pop.

The outer office was empty, but she could see one of the lines of the company phone was in use. Pop's muffled voice came to her through his closed office door. She waited until the light went out on the phone, then knocked on the door and went in.

"Nikki. How's it going?" The greeting was jovial, but Pop's green eyes were wary.

169

"Not so good, Pop. We have to talk." Nikki pulled a worn armchair closer to the desk and sat down. When she fixed him with her gaze, his eyes slid away. "I know about the deal with Archer." His face registered surprise, but he said nothing. "I was there when he called and bought you out. And I know why." Pop's eyes widened. "I know he could have put you out of business, and put you in jail into the bargain. He had the proof to do just that. And I'm the one who gave it to him."

"What do you mean?" There was a sharp edge to his voice.

"Oh, I didn't mean to do it. I was pleading your innocence with him. I showed him the company records. I believed in you, even though I had a vague feeling there was something wrong." Nikki stood up and leaned over the desk. Pop's face was closed. "You put me in a lousy position! I made a fool of myself by insisting we were innocent when we weren't!" Nikki turned from Pop's impassive face and walked around the chair. "I let Archer go over the records thinking that they would prove we *weren't* part of Grimes's scheme. They just proved how gullible I was. I thought I was a member of the family, someone you depended on. Now . . ."

Pop looked at Nikki for a long time. His gaze slid down to his hands, where he tapped a pencil nervously against his palm. Then, he said, "Girl, nobody asked you to take over the company. You just kind of did as you pleased. Oh, you did okay. You helped out when I got sick. But I figured you stayed on after that just to keep busy. I expected you'd get tired of it after awhile and go back to your painting. I only let you because you were Bob's wife. That don't mean you needed to know everything."

Nikki was incredulous. Did he think that all she'd been doing was amusing herself? If it wasn't for her the company probably wouldn't have survived. There had been no one else. . . .

That was true. But after the crisis was over, someone else could have been hired and trained. "You're just pretending at life," Julian had said.

"Look, Nikki, girl, you've got no idea what it takes to run a company like this and keep from drowning. I had to deal with Grimes or go under. If I hadn't, there were plenty of others who would. And if I made a little extra on the side, so much the better.

"So I put you in a bad spot. You didn't come out too bad. After all, old Julian Archer himself has got an eye on you. You could do a lot worse." A suggestive chuckle told Nikki what he thought about her relationship with Archer. "But you got me out of a spot. Guess I ought to thank you."

Anger swept over her like a tornado. "I don't want your thanks. I don't want anything from you. I thought that I was a Colomb, but I guess that died with Bob and I was just too blind to see it." Suddenly, the words tasted like ashes in her mouth. She wasn't really needed here. She hadn't been for a long time. She turned toward the office door.

"Nikki?"

"Goodbye, Pop."

"Miss Kate, would you *please* sit still!"

The older woman threw Nikki a withering glance. "I am sitting still. Or as still as I care to sit. At my age, it's a dangerous thing to sit too quietly. Someone is likely to come along and fling a shroud over you if you don't do more than twitch occasionally."

Nikki went on wielding her charcoal, ignoring the

acidic tone. "Well, if you must, you must. It's just that when you keep moving about so much your nose always comes out a little long. There . . . that's better," the last comment as her subject froze into position.

"Perverse child," Kate Harrison muttered under her breath. She returned her attention to the garden party invitations spread over her desk. "How many of those things are you going to do?" she asked as Nikki crumpled the page she'd been working on and began a new one.

"A few. I haven't found a pose I like," she returned.

"*You* like? But it's my portrait. Shouldn't you use the one I like?"

Nikki kept her eyes fixed on her paper, biting the inside of her cheek to hold back a smile. In the several days she'd been here, she had come to like this tart old lady and admire her zest for life. "I'm the artist," she said levelly. "The picture's mine till it's finished." She did a lightning sketch of Kate's features, focusing on bringing out her prominent bone structure and the habitual tilt of her head as she read. The line came out too strong and masculine. Nikki realized that she had unconsciously emphasized the features Kate shared with Julian. She used the top of her little finger to smudge the lines and soften the effect. Then she tore off the sheet and began another, this time exploring the way gravity and a lifetime's emotions had shaped the flesh of Kate's face.

Nikki wasn't in any hurry to begin the actual painting. She still strongly resented Julian's interference in her life. And she still didn't feel comfortable with a brush. After so many years of disuse, her skills had suffered general atrophy. Like a pianist going over the scales after a long time away from the keyboard, she was content to sketch as she restrained her muscles to obey her eye. She had begun to paint simple seascapes and landscapes as she reacquainted herself with brush and palette and relearned technique. And her excitement for it was growing.

"Have you decided on a background?" Kate asked, fixing her with a sharp black gaze.

"I don't know." Nikki shrugged noncommittally. She ripped off the page she'd been working on and dropped it on the floor with the others to be sprayed with fixative later. Picking up a rag and carefully wiping her fingers free of charcoal, she studied her subject thoughtfully for a moment.

There was the same keen intelligence in Kate's eyes as in her grandson's, but there was also a mischievous glint. The light streaming through the arched window before her chrome and glass desk gave an almost iridescent glow to Kate's Chinese blue caftan with its printed border of peacock feathers at the hem.

Nikki suspected that Kate had designed the white-on-white decor as a foil for her flamboyant self. "You should be dressed in red, of course," she said thoughtfully. Kate nodded. "And I'll paint you against a foliage and flower motif—lots of red geraniums, I think. And some deep gray shadows," she mused, ignoring the mutinous tightening of the older woman's mouth. "Or—oh, I have it! We'll dress you all in gray tones to match your hair and paint you beside a turbulent sea on a gray and stormy day . . ." Nikki snatched up the charcoal and her hand flew over the paper, capturing Kate's sardonic half-smile and the fiery spark in her black eyes that told of the devastating set down trembling on her tongue.

But the set down never came. Kate returned to her

invitations, Nikki became absorbed in adding detail to the sketch and let her guard slip.

"Julian called yesterday," Kate said. Her tone was offhand, but her eyes sparkled with interest as she watched Nikki.

The salvo was a direct hit. Nikki glanced up, then just as quickly dropped her eyes to hide the rush of emotion his name had caused. "Oh? How is Houston?"

"Europe. He went off to Europe last week to cement a couple of business deals, and I think he stayed on for a few days to relax. I thought you knew." Kate noticed that Nikki seemed intent on the page before her but the pencil wasn't moving. "You know how Julian is . . ." she went on idly, ". . . or perhaps you don't. I imagine you haven't known him that long."

Nikki recognized the barely-veiled inquiry for what it was. This wasn't the first time that Kate had tried to discover the extent of her relationship with Julian. Maybe it was time to be straightforward.

But what *was* her relationship with Julian?

She had to put an end to the budding affair. But she couldn't seem to shake her need for him. It wasn't as if he were around everyday to remind her of how she felt. Still, he seemed to be a part of everything she did. And whenever she heard his name—which, thanks to Kate, was at least a half-dozen times a day—something flip-flopped inside her. Once Kate's portrait was done and she'd gotten on with her life, maybe then he wouldn't haunt her quite so much.

Anyway, she had to let Kate know, somehow, that there was nothing between herself and Julian. Not anymore. Nikki looked up and met Kate's gaze squarely. "We've known each other just a few weeks. It seems a lot longer." She added deliberately, "I hope he's having a good time."

"Oh, I'm sure he is. He called from Felicia Grenville's Chateau. I'm not sure just where that might be. You do know who that is?"

"Yes. That English actress. The one who does those pantyhose commercials."

"Yes, that's the one. There may have been something between the two of them for a while, but I'm sure that's all over now. You needn't concern yourself that he's staying there. I'm sure it's all quite innocent." Kate's tone held a deliberate reassurance.

"Kate, there's nothing between Julian and myself." And then, to Kate's look of frank disbelief, "It seemed for awhile that something might develop, but it didn't."

"Oh?" The older woman's tone was sardonic. "Then why did he bring you here, really?"

"It's a little hard to explain. He admires the way I paint. He wants me to pursue it. I think that he was being kind. He knew I needed somewhere to sort out my life after he fired me."

"Oh, so that's how you met. You worked for him. But why did he fire you?"

"No. I met him when he fired me the first time. Or should I say, the company I worked for. Then I told him that he couldn't—and he gave me a chance to prove that we weren't involved in the embezzlement. Only we really were—and I didn't know it." Nikki sighed. "This is a little complicated."

"Not at all," Kate said dryly. "So the company you worked for was involved in that business with Grimes. And Julian broke off any dealings."

"No. He was going to, but he couldn't because I'd given him this painting he'd asked for."

"Okay," Kate said, as if Nikki's statement had made sense.

"He bought the company. Then he fired me so that I could paint your portrait for him."

"Uh, huh."

"I think it's just that I offended his sense of order, you see. You know—a round peg in a square hole."

"I see. He bought the company you worked for so that he could fire you and make you paint my portrait. But there's nothing special between you two."

"Yes!" Nikki smiled, relieved that the older woman understood. Then Kate fixed her with a doubtful black eye, and Nikki's smile faltered.

"Really, Nicole. If you didn't want to tell me, all you had to do was say so. Or at least make up a better story!" She pushed herself away from the desk. "I have to be at a meeting to organize the church bazaar. If I'm late, Laura Needham will be trying to run everyone." With that, Kate rose and swept regally from the room.

"Wait! What about the sketches? And when shall I plan to start the painting?"

"Later," Kate called over her shoulder as she turned down the hall. "And don't you dare add one millimeter to my nose!" Then she disappeared in a swirl of iridescent blue.

"When?" Nikki asked, cradling the telephone on her shoulder as she viciously cleared turpentine from the paintbrush by rapping it against the leg of the easel. The furniture in the upstairs bedroom had been pushed back out of harm's way, and newspapers were spread out to protect the floor. "Kate, you promised you'd sit this afternoon. I should have known better than to get everything ready before I had you lashed to a chair."

"I'm sorry," the older woman said. "I forgot that this was the afternoon of the church bazaar. I really must be here. You know, they say that the short-term memory is the first thing to go . . .''

"When?" Nikki repeated. "I want to finish your hands."

"I have seven age spots on the right, and five on the left. Use your imagination. Or maybe you could finish the background."

The background was nearly finished. She'd decided to paint Kate with her forearms resting on her modern acrylic desk where she sat each morning to answer her correspondence and arrange her social affairs. Nikki would include a little of the naked arched window which was at a right angle to the desk. A finely-tooled leather volume could be reflected in the acrylic surface of the desk beside Kate's gold pen and pencil set. Kate would, of course, wear a caftan, this one of mauve, purple, silver, and fawn stripes. In her mind, Nikki could already see the curves and lines of the fabric drape.

"No, Kate. I can't work on the background. Please try to understand." Nikki sighed. "I've been here almost a month, and—well, it's just time to finish this and get on with my life." There. She'd said it. Her first open acknowledgment that it was time to leave.

"Oh? You have commitments? Plans?"

"Well, no. Not exactly." Nikki really didn't know where she was going. She'd started out several times to form some plan of action, then Kate would call over to the guest house and invite her for afternoon coffee or to go along on some outing or other. This had happened quite often lately. "But I *do* have to make some. Kate, I can't stay here indefinitely!"

"And why not? This is where Julian brought you. And when you two have patched up the squabble that has you both on your high horses . . ."

"Kate!" Nikki gasped in exasperation. Telling Kate that there was nothing between herself and Julian had definitely been the wrong tack. Now the older woman seemed convinced that they were bound for the altar. "Either you schedule several afternoons next week to sit for me and nail yourself to that chair, or I'll have no choice but to work on the background—and change it to a livid chartreuse."

"Blackmailer! All right. After the garden party. But I'll have to check my calendar to be certain. Now, as to the reason for my call—we're a bit shorthanded down here, and I was wondering . . ."

She sighed resignedly as Kate went on to outline just how much Nikki was needed to help out. "Okay, Kate," she agreed. "But you'll have to send someone to get me. My car's in the shop, remember? And it's Cindy's day off."

Nikki smiled as she hung up the receiver. The older woman always managed to have things precisely her own way.

Nikki's gaze was drawn back to the canvas. The excitement was there. An overview of exactly how the painting should look formed inside her head. She had all the sketches she'd done—taped now to the walls near her easel. She probably needed Kate to sit for her only half as often as she'd said. But then it was doubtful that Kate would sit for her half as many times as she'd asked.

There had been a time when Nikki might have worked from the sketches. But though the excitement was back, she felt a niggling doubt. She'd feel more confident if she had Kate seated before her for the real work.

As Nikki began tucking away her paints in the large

tackle box that she'd bought to store them, the phone rang again. "Harrison residence," she answered.

There was a slight pause. "Nicole?"

It was Julian's voice. Nikki's heart began to race at the sound of it.

"Hello," she said softly. "How . . . how are you?"

"Fine." Was there an edge of fatigue in his voice? "How is the painting coming along?" He did sound tired.

"Underway." Nikki's violet eyes went back to the canvas with the main figure only a blocked-in form. "But progressing slowly. Your grandmother is as hard to pin down as quicksilver." She paused a moment as his subdued chuckle came to her over the line. "She's not here, by the way."

"I'm not surprised. I'll catch her next time." There was a pause. "Nikki . . . how are you?"

Nikki closed her eyes and let the caring in his deep voice soothe her. At least they could be friends. "Everything is going well," she said with a brightness she didn't really feel. "I'm enjoying doing this portrait. Kate's a special person." Her heart wasn't in this. "I still have some decisions to make—what I'll do after it's finished and all that—but the important thing is I'm excited by painting again." There. That's what he wanted to hear.

"Nikki, I asked how *you* are. You haven't answered my question."

"Oh . . ." She caught her bottom lip beneath her teeth. She couldn't tell him that she ached with loneliness for him, how she longed to see him, touch him, be with him. "There's nothing wrong with me that time won't cure," she answered cryptically, and hoped that it was the truth. "Julian, there is something. Your grandmother doesn't understand how things are between us. And the more I try to explain to her that our relationship didn't work out, the more convinced she becomes that we're headed for the altar.

"Your Aunt Clara and one of her daughters were here to visit a couple of days ago, and Kate gave them the impression that we had only to set the date. Then this morning, your Uncle Elliot gave me this big bear hug and welcomed me to the family." Nikki gave a great heaving sigh. "Could you try to clear this up? I mean, before Kate starts sending out engagement announcements?"

Julian's words were clipped. "I'll see what I can do."

"Thank you. I really do like your grandmother. I just don't want her harboring any misconceptions."

"Okay, Nikki. Tell Kate that I'm in Denmark right now, but that I plan to be back in the States in a few more days. She can reach me through the office if she needs me. And, Nikki . . . take care."

"You, too."

"Damn," Nikki said softly after replacing the phone in its cradle. How could she have known she'd miss him this much. "Damn."

"I don't know why I let you talk me into this," Nikki grumbled as she bent over to tie her shoe by the side of a quiet residential street. Then she yelped in pain as she discovered that she had inadvertently stopped in a fire ant trail. By the time she'd beaten off the feisty creatures and smashed two that had seized her shin beneath the leg of her jeans, Kate was a good hundred yards ahead.

"Hurry up, slowpoke!" Kate called to her. "I swear! You make *me* feel young."

"We could be working on your portrait! This is the

first time in two days that you've been free," Nikki panted as she jogged to catch up.

"I told you that I'll sit when we get back."

"All this exercise has made your cheeks flushed," Nikki protested. "Your skin tone's all wrong."

"Listen. At my age, one is grateful for any sign of circulation one can get!" Kate snapped sardonically.

They continued in silence for a few minutes, past houses set back from the street behind tall pines and lush landscaped yards. Nikki had discovered that there were primarily two different types of residents in the area: retirees; and executives, who commuted to New Orleans. Kate was the unofficial social spokesperson for the retirees, while her arch-rival and next door neighbor, Laura Needham, held the same position among the executives' wives.

Nikki smiled, remembering how surprised she'd been earlier when Kate had appeared on the deck of the guest house in hot-pink jogging togs and matching high-tops—only minutes before Nikki had scheduled her for a sitting. Nikki knew perfectly well that Kate walked, according to her doctor's instructions, every morning, usually quite early. Nikki had often accompanied her. But Kate had insisted that she had missed her walk this morning and simply *had* to get it out of the way.

That Laura and Neal Needham were standing on the dock next door, admiring their new Egg Harbor yacht was purely coincidental, of course.

"Mrs. Harrison! Ahoy!" Laura Needham called, waving. "Come and see Neal's new toy!"

"Braggart," Kate said under her breath as she threw the couple a saccharine smile and waved back. "I'm surprised the *Queen Mary* drafts that shallow. Come, Nicole. Since they've blown a fortune on that thing, I suppose politeness dictates that we go ooh and ahh."

Nikki followed with a smile, more curious about what Kate was up to than about the boat.

Laura Needham showed them the plush lounge and cleverly designed galley. Then, as Laura led Kate away to the main stateroom, Nikki followed Neal to the engine compartment where they examined the gleaming, new twin-diesel engines and talked clutches and reduction.

"Permission to come aboard?" a pleasantly southern male voice called from somewhere outside.

"Sounds like my son, Chuck." Neal smiled, then called, "We're on our way out!"

Back on deck, Neal introduced her to a tall blonde man with a suntanned face. Crinkles appeared at the corners of his electric-blue eyes as he smiled. Nikki decided she was seeing the image of Neal thirty years earlier.

"Hello," Chuck said as he shook her hand, interest showing in his friendly smile. "Dad, I wouldn't tell Mom that you were down there checking out the engines, if I were you. Ms. Duval is much too pretty for Mom to buy it."

Neal laughed and clapped his son on the back. "Your chauvinism is showing. Nikki was telling me about the engines in the boats she piloted in her former job." Neal turned back to Nikki. "Chuck is just a landlubbing veterinarian."

"Really? A lady captain?" The interest was growing.

"Much too grand a title," Nikki protested, liking his easy smile, though it didn't do the things to her that Julian's did. "Taxi driver would be more accurate— mostly in protected inland waters and bays. There was very little navigation involved—at least not of the sort that will be required for the trip that Neal and Laura are planning to take to Fort Walton Beach. I think being a veterinarian must be much more interesting.''

"I could tell you about it over supper one evening,'' Chuck suggested.

Nikki decided this would be just the thing to put Kate's assumptions to rest. She opened her mouth to accept the invitation when she heard:

"I see you've met my grandson's fiancée.''

Kate and Laura appeared from inside the cabin. Nikki shot Kate a dark look. "Kate, Julian and I are not engaged.''

"Sorry, dear. I forgot. You're *not* engaged.'' Kate patted Nikki's hand, then turned to the rest of the assembly. "I don't know why they insist on keeping it a secret.''

Nikki turned back to Chuck with her acceptance on her lips, but at his questioning look managed only an apologetic smile. She would have been going out with him only to thwart Kate, not out of any real interest. That wouldn't have been fair. He seemed much too nice for that.

Nikki moved away and down the short gangway to the floating dock. She turned to help steady Kate.

"Wonderful boat, Laura. I *am* sorry you'll miss the garden party,'' Kate said over her shoulder to the woman following close behind. Behind her glasses Laura Needham's eyes found Nikki's and her wry smile said that she knew very well how Kate felt about her coming absence.

"We'll be back afterward for . . . ah, whatever else is happening. Neal has another thought coming if he thinks I'm going to miss all of the better parties this spring.'' A look passed between the two women that Nikki couldn't interpret.

Then Laura resumed hostilities as she turned to Nikki

with a smile and asked, "How is the portrait coming? I was very impressed by the sketches Mrs. Harrison showed us at the ladies' club meeting the other night. I was wondering—when you've finished the one of Kate—would you paint a picture of Chuck?"

Laura's eyes twinkled as Kate announced that they really must get on with their walk, grabbed Nikki's arm, and dragged her away before she could answer.

"I remember when this was all woodland," Kate said, recalling Nikki to the present. She surveyed the surrounding homes. "When Julian was a boy he loved to hike here with his grandfather. The woods grew all the way back to the bayou. Sometimes, they'd take Julian's little two-man tent and camp out on a sandbar overnight and fish."

Kate paused by a large, empty corner lot, panting from exertion. Nikki, who wasn't in the least tired, realized with a slight shock that Kate's appearance of boundless energy was a sham.

"Richard loved all his grandchildren, but he doted on Joan's boys. Particularly Julian. I suppose I do, too." Kate went on when she had regained her breath. "This is where the old house used to stand—before Hurricane Camille. I didn't want to rebuild in the same place."

Nikki noticed that it wasn't just an empty lot. Hidden in the midst of the wild hedge and undergrowth were brick pillars that once must have supported a house. She remembered other bare slabs and steps that led to nowhere, particularly in Gulfport and Biloxi on lots facing the beach.

Kate sighed, and seated herself on one of the pillars. "I still own this property. I guess I always hoped Julian would settle down and build a home here one day. He could move his corporate headquarters to New Orleans.

Now that Richard's gone, well . . . I guess you could say that it's my last wish before I die.''

"Just a little too thick, Kate," Nikki said dryly. "But I do have to say that brave-but-fading look was worthy of Sarah Bernhardt."

Kate chuckled. "I always thought that I should have had a career on the stage. No bite, huh?"

"Not a nibble."

Kate smiled ruefully. "Can't blame me for trying." She rose and began walking again, not quite as briskly as before.

Kate was almost at a loss as to what to do with the pair. Here was this girl who glowed every time Julian's name was mentioned, then turned a dismal gray and went into a denial routine. Then there was that silly grandson of hers, leaving the girl here for weeks on end without ever coming back to watch out for his interest or work out whatever was keeping them apart. He deserved for someone like Chuck Needham to come along and snatch her away!

Idiots! Letting time slip away from them like that.

Although it went against her grain, Kate decided to try the direct approach. "All bluffs aside, Nicole, I've grown very fond of you. I would like to see you and my grandson married before they come and haul me away."

"Kate . . . Gram," Nikki's eyes were beseeching, "why are you always making jokes about dying?"

Kate seemed surprised. "Do I? I suppose for the same reason that we joke about anything—to get used to concepts that are a little too shattering when faced head-on. Like old age and death."

"You aren't really old," Nikki protested.

"I'm eighty-two. That's only middle-aged if one lives to be a hundred sixty-four." The old woman smiled wryly. "Now stop skirting the subject. What about you and Julian?"

"Marriage has never been mentioned between us," Nikki admitted softly.

"You mean he wants you to live with him? That's not like Julian," Kate said almost to herself, shaking her head. "If he cared enough to make a commitment, I'd have bet he'd make it a complete one." She shook her head as if puzzled. They walked on in silence.

"Good, we're almost home," Kate said, breathing heavily as they started up the drive. "I'll shower and change while you set up your materials, if you think we have the time before the light fades."

Nikki cast a glance at the sun. "We could squeeze in about an hour. You mean you're *volunteering* to sit?"

"Of course. There's the garden party the day after tomorrow, but after that I should have plenty of time to sit. We have to get this picture finished, you know, so that it has time to dry and go to the framer's before—" Kate breezed past her through the door, leaving the statement unfinished.

Nikki paused, looking after her. There was a sinking feeling in the pit of her stomach. "Kate," Nikki called, following the woman into the house. "I've had the distinct impression the last few days that something's going on that I should know about." But Kate had disappeared inside. There was no answer. Nikki sighed, and went to set up her paints.

THIRTEEN

Nikki walked into the kitchen of the main house just in time to take the screaming tea-kettle off the stove.

"Cindy?" she called. There was no answer. The tea pot stood ready on the tray beside the sugar and cream containers. Nikki added another cup and saucer to the one already on the tray and fetched the plate of lemon slices from the refrigerator. After pouring the hot water over the tea bags in the pot, she carried the tray into the den.

"Kate, your tea's ready. Where is Cindy?"

Kate looked up from her place on the low sofa. "Nikki, dear, how nice. Cindy went to the market. I'd forgotten that she put the kettle on before she left." Her usually bright eyes sparkled with a hint of mischief. "Come, join me. Put the tray here." Kate picked up two large volumes that rested on the low table in front of the sofa. "And sit down with me." She patted the seat next to her.

"Okay, Kate, what's up?"

"Why, I was only sitting here reminiscing. And looking at these old photos." A large photo album was opened across her lap.

Nikki fixed them each a cup of tea and leaned back as Kate leafed through the pages of the album. Some of the photos were very old.

"This is my mother and father on their wedding day," Kate said. "You can see how much I resemble my father. He was an old bore, not able to accept change. Mama straightened him out over the years." She caressed the old photograph lovingly. "They didn't have much, but I don't ever remember being unhappy." Kate leafed through a few more pages to the black and white photo of a stern-faced young woman in a long dress. "That's me, Nikki, all dressed up for some cotillion. My mother insisted that I attend all the best dances. I was about as attractive as a horse. She'd have fainted if she'd known that I spent the time at those dances sitting in a corner. She was determined that I should meet a 'nice' young man. Nice meant wealthy. But I had my own way in the end. I met Richard Harrison." Kate indicated a faded photograph of a tall young man with a beautiful smile and sparkling light eyes. "He was a charmer, my Richard. He had girls leaning on his arm everywhere he went. But when I saw him, I knew that he would be my husband. There was no question in my mind." Kate's eyes were soft with his memory. Her face glowed. "He used to call me his queen." She chuckled. "He said that the first time he saw me he thought I must be royalty, I walked so proud. He said all those soft, fluttery girls he'd been dating were like peasants beside me. After that, he never looked at another girl." She turned the page to the wedding photo. The expression on the face of the young woman in the picture was beatific. This was Kate in love. *Is this how I look at Julian?* Nikki thought.

Kate turned pages showing herself and Richard with their children. Nikki's eyes kept being drawn back to the rather sullen little girl who had grown up to be Julian's mother. There was almost a hunted look about the child, and the photos that showed her smiling were few.

"Joan was such a ninny," Kate said. "And I never gave her a chance." Regret colored her voice. "I guess I always overshadowed Joan. I wanted her to be just like me. That's usually a male failing. But I could see the weakness in her and it irked me. I drove her—until I drove her away. She ran off with Craig Archer when she was sixteen and she's been trying to be happy ever since." Kate slowly turned a few more pages that showed the young couple with their two small sons. The woman's face was smiling but her eyes still held that concerned look. "Craig wasn't a bad man. And I think he truly loved Joan, in his way. But he'd grown up poor, and his whole life revolved around making money. So Joan tried to gain approval the only way she could; by becoming the perfect corporate wife. It was a job she was never cut out for." She gazed at a photo of the young mother stiffly holding a baby while a small boy stood beside her. "She was never much of a mother," Kate said softly. "But then, she didn't have much to go by."

Nikki reached out and put her hand on Kate's arm. The older woman came out of reverie and smiled ruefully. "I guess I do this every once in a while just to bring myself back to earth. I tend to get too big for my britches. It reminds me that I mustn't meddle."

There seemed to be a lot of photos of the two boys. Some included other children. "One of my sons lived in Biloxi for a few years," Kate said. "When Frank and Julian came here for summer vacation, Jim's boys would come, too. Richard loved it." She chuckled and shook her head. "I was the only female around and they sure kept me hopping. Then Sara started coming, too.'' Kate pointed to a photograph of the five boys—ranging in age from about thirteen to about eight—in which there was also a small freckled, pigtailed girl. ''She showed those boys a thing or two. She was a better fisherman than any of them. I guess because she could keep still better and didn't scare the fish away.'' Kate turned the page to show Nikki a picture of the girl lifting a gigantic catfish with the help of a slender boy with intense gray eyes. ''I think Julian was the only one of the boys who gave Sara credit for being an equal.''

Nikki was concentrating on the face of that intense little boy as the pages were turned. There were shots where his face reflected only the joy of a child engaged in pursuits dear to his heart; hunting, fishing, swimming, roughhousing with friends. But there were times that the faded color snapshots showed the single-minded determination that would take him to success as a man. And, in the face of his grandfather, a pride and realization that this boy was special.

Kate watched Nikki's face as she gave special attention to the photos of Julian and his grandfather. She could see the searching that was going on in Nikki's mind to find the real Julian, to gain an insight into the man by learning about the boy. She continued her explanation in a voice softened by her affection for this young woman who had stolen Julian's heart—and her own. ''Richard seemed to see something in Julian that Craig never took the time to see. Of course, Craig was always too busy to see that his family needed him.'' She turned the pages to scenes from a family Christmas. ''Julian was fourteen that year. He had just started that outrageous growth spurt and he looked terribly thin. Craig wasn't there, of course. He never seemed to make it for the holidays. There was always some business deal to take care of. It made it much worse for Julian because his birthday is the day after Christmas. I think he felt doubly deserted. Frank was the only son to Craig then. Not just because he was the oldest, but because Frank was the image of his father. Julian took after our side of the family in appearance, but he is very like his father in other ways. He has a tendency to forget that people have needs sometimes." *Would Nikki understand what she was trying to tell her?* "But when he cares for someone he can never do enough for them. In a lot of ways, he learned from his father's mistakes. Of course, he picked up a few of my bad habits, too."

Nikki looked at Kate with a knowing smile on her face. Yes, Julian and his grandmother were alike in some things. Like maneuvering people into doing what they felt was the right thing, sometimes despite that person's wishes. "Kate, there is something I don't understand. If Julian's father ignored him so much as a child and chose Frank to be his heir, why was Julian ready to step into Archer Oil when Frank wouldn't? It seems that there would be too much resentment against his father's neglect."

"Ah, yes," Kate murmured. "There was. But Julian had always been his father's son. Craig had been too blind to see it." The older woman looked at Nikki thoughtfully. "He had wanted his father's approval all his life, and I think he'd felt that he'd never achieved it. I think that resentment spawned a determination to out-do Craig's achievements. Julian did the only thing he could to get back at Craig—he became a success."

As the pages of his life were turned for her, Nikki saw the playful youngster become a solemn young man and then a confident adult. But in the family photos he always seemed to be in the rear—and separate, somehow. The only pictures that showed him relaxed and a part of the group were the ones with his grandparents. It was clear that Richard and Kate had, in a sense, become the parents he had needed.

Nikki listened with only half an ear as Kate rambled on about the events depicted in the album. Her mind kept going back to the Julian Archer she knew, and the one she had discovered within the pages of the album. A deep aching filled her. This man had overcome things as painful as those she had experienced. And he had come out of them stronger, and with more compassion than anyone could have expected.

Her eyes focused on the pictures Kate was displaying. It was apparently a fairly recent Christmas. Kate's living room was decorated with garlands of flocked greenery, and in the corner was a huge flocked tree adorned with silver and blue ornaments. A series of photos showed family members opening gifts. A man, whom, from the photos of them as children, she recognized as Julian's brother Frank, sat next to a pretty girl with soft brown hair and eyes. In the girl's lap was a darling dark-haired baby. The baby was looking at the person operating the camera. A bright smile showed two tiny teeth, and the corners of the eyes were crinkled. And the baby's eyes were silver gray.

Something caught her eye and drew it back to the left hand corner of the picture. A familiar dark head was there, bent over a blonde one. Her heart lurched when she realized who it was. This had been Julian's wife.

Nikki's gaze returned to Julian's face. He was smiling down at the beautiful woman and his face . . . She had seen that look on his face, when he had looked at her.

He had looked at his wife with those eyes full of

wanting. And she could hear the indifference in his voice when he had spoken of Katrina and how little the marriage had meant to him, eventually.

Nikki stood up abruptly, her eyes clouded with the tears that had been so close to the surface all day. She snatched up the tray with its discarded cups and turned toward the kitchen.

"Nicole . . . ?"

"Kate . . . I . . . uh," Nikki stammered. "I . . . just remembered there's something I have to do." She kept her head averted from Kate's sharp black eyes. "I'll talk to you later."

Kate recognized the pleading tone. "That's all right, dear. I understand." She watched Nikki's stiff back disappear into the kitchen. "Damn, Julian Archer!" she muttered. "It's time you did something about this!"

"Perfectly lovely weather." A matron in pearls and a wide-brimmed hat smiled at Nikki and went about selecting several finger sandwiches from those arranged on the outdoor buffet. "I really don't know how Katherine always has such lovely weather for her affairs."

"Because Katherine wouldn't stand for anything less!" said the lady at her elbow. The speaker's eyes twinkled behind designer-framed bifocals.

This drew smiles and chuckles from everyone who heard, including Kate, who declared, "Quite right, Mildred. I always prefer to get my way," before moving away to greet some late arrivals to the already crowded garden.

Kate looks especially pretty today, Nikki thought, watching her play hostess. The drop waisted middy-style suit, with its shiny, brass-buttoned white jacket and precisely-pleated skirt of navy blue might have been straight out of the 1920s.

"Excuse me, my dear, could you tell me what filling Kate has in these little pastry cups?" a lady with blue-tinted hair asked Nikki.

"Crab, I think, ma'am," Nikki answered.

"Is it the Altar Society I remember you from? Or the Blood Drive Volunteers?" the woman asked.

"Neither, ma'am," Nikki answered with a smile.

"No, this is Julian's young lady. She's been spending some time with Kate," another lady put in, one Nikki recognized vaguely. Kate had so many friends it was hard to keep them straight. "Remember," the woman continued, "she drove Kate to the garden club meeting last week."

Lifting a cup of coffee in its saucer, Nikki forced a smile and began to edge away from the press. She didn't feel up to trying to explain, once again, that she was not "Julian's young lady." In fact, she thought, if one more person wished her happiness, or asked the wedding date, she might do something stupid. Like burst into tears.

Nikki made her way through the gate and wandered down the hillside. There were fewer people here, most strolling along the sandstone pathways admiring the terraced beds of annuals which were planted in red and white. A light breeze tugged at the full skirt of her mint-green linen dress.

As Nikki's violet gaze skimmed over the quiet waters, she wondered where Julian was and what he was doing. She had never known before that it was possible to miss anyone so completely. Without him the world seemed, somehow, colorless; more colorless than it had before her art had returned.

"Nicole, dear, there's someone I want you to meet." Kate called from the courtyard gate. Nikki plastered a smile on her face and walked back up the hill.

"Nicole, this is Evelyn Bass." Kate presented her to a diminutive woman, who was easily several years older than Kate. Her skin was crinkled finely like crushed ivory satin, her hair pure white. She had a dowager's hump and stood with the aid of a cane. But her eyes, behind gold-rimmed glasses, were lively as they studied Nikki.

"So you're the young genius Kate has been telling me about. The one who is painting her portrait," the old lady said, her eyes twinkling.

Nikki flushed to the roots of her hair. "The portrait isn't finished," she managed to stammer. Then the name Evelyn Bass registered and she shot Kate a glowering look. "I've always admired your watercolors, Ms. Bass. I have several prints from your wildflower series at home. Your plants appear so delicate and fragile. It makes me think of how delicate our whole ecology truly is."

"Thank you, dear." Ms. Bass moved her cane from one hand to the other and flexed her fingers, her expression rueful. "But I'm afraid that age and arthritis are limiting me these days. I envy you—your youth and your gift. Now, don't put up any false modesty," she forestalled as Nikki began to protest. "I know that Kate is prejudiced because you're Julian's fiancée, but she has shown me some of your work. Did I say something wrong?"

"Nicole?" the lady Nikki remembered as Mildred asked as she joined the group, her friend in the wide-brimmed hat in tow. "When did you say that you've set the day? My word! Look who's here!"

Nikki turned as a shadow fell over her and looked up into a familiar pair of gray eyes. Her heart leaped into her throat and, although she couldn't know it, into her eyes. Looking into them, Julian felt a surge of hope.

"I was just asking your fiancée about the date of the wedding." Mildred redirected her question to Julian.

Nikki's look implored him to rescue her. It was more than Julian could resist. He handed a startled Mildred the jacket he'd been carrying over his shoulder, then pulled Nikki to him with an arm around her waist and slipped the other behind her shoulders. Then he bent her backwards in a kiss that put Evelyn vividly in mind of Rudolf Valentino.

Nikki resisted until Julian's mouth touched hers.

Then her hand slipped up his back, glorying in the feel of his tensed muscles as she molded her body more perfectly to his. She angled her head, offering her mouth to his tongue. His tongue took immediate possession of it and the strength of the reaction erupting within her made her tremble.

Nikki's eyes flew open as Julian broke away, and she looked up into eyes and a face as filled with need as her own. Then the expression was gone and he was steadying her on her feet to a chorus of old-lady titters and a scattering of applause. Nikki looked about her at the sea of smiling faces. Her stricken eyes moved back to Julian. Then she turned and hurried away.

A stiff breeze caused the brightly colored sail to snap as Julian brought the catamaran around to tack toward the east. Nikki closed her eyes and leaned back against the canvas deck, the sun warming her skin.

When Julian had arrived yesterday, all the feeling that she thought she'd mastered had come rushing back. This morning, he had asked her to go sailing with him and she had almost refused. The thought of being alone with him again had been disturbing.

So why *had* she come? The truth was she just couldn't resist being with him.

Nikki opened her eyes in little slits, watching Julian. A quiver of excitement ran through her as he leaned back over the water, his arm and shoulder muscles delineated by the tension he kept on the line. Hair-dusted pectorals and belly muscles rippled as he secured the rope.

Julian's trip out of the country must have taken him to the south of France, she thought. A tan like that wasn't acquired in boardrooms. Why did he have to look so damn sexy! That tiny little suit—very European. The sides of the aqua spandex garment were barely an inch wide. His flat abdomen with its indented navel, his firm thighs—he looked like a diet soda ad. Except for that face, she thought as he tilted his head back like a sun-worshipper. Too strong a face, and not boy-pretty enough to be a model's. But the warmth in his gray eyes as he smiled at her caused a little flip-flop in her belly.

Stop it! Nikki admonished herself. He's *not* for you. She turned over to toast her other side and gazed out over the Sound.

Little whitecaps formed as gusts of wind peaked the water. The sun dazzled the blueness into diamond sparkles. Green shoreline rose to an expanse of blue sky that was dotted by puffs that sailed toward the horizon. Kate's house was a dot of white peeking out of green.

Julian's face grew dark and brooding as he looked at Nikki stretched out on the canvas. Ever since he'd arrived yesterday she had been keeping distance between them. It had been a mistake to tease her with that impulsive kiss but the situation had been irresistible. Then she had responded—and it hadn't been a joke anymore. And, of course, she had reacted by running away and staying away all evening.

Julian tossed the anchor over the side as the boat neared one of the islands rimming the Sound. He asked, "Want to go for a swim?"

Nikki turned over and sat up. Her eyes were like a reflection of the cloudy water. She smiled tentatively. "The water looks good." She dropped her feet over the side. "It's safe this far out, isn't it? I mean—no sharks or anything?" At the menacing look he gave her, she quickly pulled her feet out of the water. Julian roared with laughter at her little-girl look of fear.

The laughter seemed to release something that had been coiled tightly within him. "No, Nikki. At least not the finny kind." He gave her a sharkish smile and shoved her unceremoniously into the water.

Nikki came up sputtering to find Julian standing on the bobbing deck, hands on hips and legs spread, still laughing. He looked like some malicious god.

"Arrogant . . . !" Nikki grumbled, and gave the hull a shove. It rocked dangerously, and Nikki crowed with merriment as Julian windmilled his arms, ineffectually trying to balance himself, then whirled and splashed into the drink. But the wave from his entry caught Nikki open-mouthed, and she swallowed water.

Julian broke the surface and looked around for Nikki. She wasn't in sight. Suddenly, the gleam of skin showed underwater and she burst through. His laughter changed to stomach-clenching fear as he took in the purple cast of her skin, her eyes bulging with strain as she tried to draw breath.

Quickly Julian pulled her to him. His strong arm cut the water as he dragged her back to the boat. With a hard thrust, he heaved her half onto the canvas and, steadying the bobbing hull, pulled himself up beside her.

Nikki was choking. She dragged desperately at each breath, but each cough expelled more air than she had managed to inhale. A flash of remembered terror gripped her as darkness threatened. She rose to her knees slapping the deck with her hands as she tried to use her fading strength to regain control.

A sudden blow to her back sent her flying. But when she breathed in again, it was easier. The hovering blackness receded as Nikki was able to cough up the rest of the water. As her ragged breathing slowed, she turned her head toward Julian, who was beside her rubbing her back. His face was taut. Fear was etched into his features.

"Dear God, I'm sorry." Concern roughened his voice.

"It's okay," she gasped as she rolled onto her back. A fresh fit of coughing shook her for a few moments. She still felt a bit green from the briny water she'd swallowed. "It was my own damn fault," she said, seeing how regretful he was. Then, almost to herself, "I always seem to get myself in trouble." Her tone became ironic. "Like—in over my head."

Julian grimaced at the terrible pun. "At least you still have your sense of humor."

"Yeah," she said ruefully, sitting up and rubbing her back between her shoulders. "And a lovely purple souvenir, too, I'll bet."

"I am sorry, Nikki." She looked at him sharply. His tone told her he meant more than just the near drowning. He searched her face, a strange expression shadowing his eyes. "I know I haven't made things very easy for you." He smiled ruefully. "I'm not good at losing, Nikki. Or at giving up."

She held her right hand out to him. "Okay. Friends?" He stared at her for a moment. Conflicting emotions chased each other over his face. Then a slow smile curved his mouth and lightened his eyes. Grasping her outstretched hand he pulled her toward him until his lips were just an inch from hers. His eyes held a challenge. "Want to try again?" The teasing words puffed sensitizing breaths over her mouth. Then he slipped over the side into the water. "Come on. I'll be right beside you."

An impish grin spread over her face as she got to her feet. "Not for long!" she yelled. With a lunging dive she was past him. She raced through the water, enjoying the feel of her muscles stretched to their limits, and the new easiness between Julian and herself. But as Julian swam past his leg brushed hers and she floundered in a wave of desire from the contact. She realized regretfully that she could never be detached enough with him to be just friends.

Nikki stroked toward the boat. Her mind was flooded with pictures from that weekend—was it only five weeks ago? If it were only physical, she thought, I could deal with it. She looked back, watched Julian's feet disappear as he dove under the waves.

It was more. Too much more.

Julian suddenly appeared beside her. Clutching one of the slim hulls, he said, "You never told me—have you decided what you'll do next? You must have some plans for the future." The boat dipped and bobbed with the rolling water.

Nikki grabbed the hull near him. There was a note in his voice she couldn't quite decipher. "Two of Kate's friends have offered me commissions," she said thoughtfully. "I've been thinking of accepting them. Kate showed me a darling little beach house across the bay in Pass Christian. The living area would make a good studio. It has lots of windows." Julian pushed off from the boat, treading water. When he didn't comment, she continued, "I'd like to stay near Kate. She's become a very special friend—your grandmother is a remarkable woman."

"Isn't she?" Julian's tone was distracted, but something in it caused Nikki to look sharply at him. He turned away into a suddenly cool breeze. It was a dark blue-bottomed cloud which had caught his attention as it appeared around the point of the island. The water around them turned lead gray as its mountainous top hid the sun and cats-paws played across the tops of the waves.

"We'd better head in," he decided. Julian hauled himself onto the deck. A worried frown tightened his features as he helped Nikki on board and into a life jacket. She scuttled aside while he silently shrugged into his, and tried to make herself as unobtrusive as possible as Julian gave his whole attention to maneuvering the small craft in the suddenly choppy waters. She cast a longing look northward at the shore as the boat swung 'round. It seemed so far away.

Within a minute, it was obvious that the thunderstorm was overtaking them. They would never make it. Lightning streaked to a point about a hundred yards off the bow. Thunder boomed and Nikki shrieked, covering her ears.

"I'm going to turn it toward that little island to the east," Julian shouted above the next rumble. "There used to be an old shack on it. But you'll have to help me counter balance when I turn the boat or we'll capsize. Okay?"

Nikki nodded. The sail swung around and snapped full. Nikki scrambled to the port side and, catching the line, hung out over the water as far as she dared. In a few moments, the cat had run up onto the beach, just as the first slashing drops of rain splattered down on them.

"Are you all right?" Julian lifted her against his broad chest. His voice was whipped away by the force of the wind.

"Yes!" Nikki pushed her hair out of her eyes and looked around. A stand of scrub pine grew about thirty yards up the beach. "There!" She twisted out of Julian's grasp and began to run toward it.

Another blinding flash of lightning exploded, followed instantly by a deafening crash that shook the ground. Nikki threw her hands over her ears, clenched her eyes tight, and dropped to her knees in the sand. A piercing shriek tore from her throat.

Julian was dazed for a moment. Spots of light danced before his eyes as he searched frantically for Nikki. His hands found her before his eyes did. He scooped her into his arms, heading for the outline of a shack a short way up the beach. The hut had only three walls intact. Planks from the fourth lay scattered down to the water. The rain pounded ominously on the rusted, misshapen tin roof, but the sand floor was dry. Julian dropped to his knees, placing Nikki on hers in the sand. Nikki came to at the sound of Julian's voice calling her name. His grip on her arms hurt. But the terror that had overtaken her was slowly diminishing. And Julian's words penetrated.

"Nikki. It's okay now. Open your eyes. Look at me." The strange wailing noise that had accompanied the sound of wind and rain stopped, and she realized that it had been coming from her.

"I'm sorry. I'm such a coward."

"It's okay. Be as frightened as you want." Julian

untied the beach towel he had knotted around her waist and pulled it up over her shoulders. Water ran from her hair down over her face, and he brushed the drops away.

Another flash of brightness and thunderclap split the air. Nikki cringed, whimpering.

"Nikki. It's okay." Julian's grip on her arms tightened again. She looked at him, her eyes pleading.

"I . . . I'm afraid."

"Don't think about it." His fingers deftly released her life jacket, pulled it down her arms. He ran his fingers gently back up them to cup her face, forcing her eyes away from the dreaded storm, to look into his. "Just think about me."

FOURTEEN

Julian's eyes captured hers. The worry in them gradually changed to warmth. Another flash of light illumi-
nated his features. His mouth held the hint of a smile,
the ends of his mustache just barely tilting upwards. A
small crease divided his forehead between his eyebrows. His dark thick hair was rumpled and wet around
his face. His eyes glowed with some strange inner light.
Nikki felt drawn into them, held gently. The rage of
the storm seemed distant, unreal. The spasms that had
racked her subsided as a consuming warmth took hold
of her.

Nikki raised her hands to cover the ones that still
held her face. There was such tenderness in the way he
touched her, such ardor in the gray eyes that smiled
into hers. A deep calm filled her even as the look in
his eyes kindled a fire inside her. She was safe here
with Julian. As long as he looked at her that way,
nothing could hurt her.

She slid her hands down Julian's arms to his shoulders. The skin felt warm, pliant, over the firmness of
his muscles. His hands, fallen to her towel-covered

shoulders, burned through the terry cloth. She moved her hands to the catch of his life vest. Without taking her eyes from him, she unfastened it. She was marginally aware that, as she slipped it from his shoulders, her towel was falling to the sand. But she could not take her eyes from the magnetic look that held her.

The rhythmic slash of the rain on the roof seemed to echo the pounding of the blood in her ears, and the beat of Julian's heart under her fingers. His hands against her coolness, her cool fingers on the burning swell of his chest, seemed to focus the distance between them. She was not aware of closing the distance, of sliding her arms around him, of pulling his heat against her. She only knew she sought his lips with a need that seemed to draw every cell of her toward him. The moment his lips claimed hers, opening and drinking in her desire, Nikki knew this was where she had to be. Time didn't matter. Security didn't matter. All that mattered was being with Julian. Feeling alive as she felt now. Tomorrow . . . she'd think about all the reasons it wouldn't work. Now, time lost all meaning. The storm rumbling in the background became unreal. The feel of Julian's hands, Julian's lips, Julian's hard, lean body was all that existed. Every movement was infinitely slow. Every contact between their bodies was electric, riveting. And through all of it, Nikki couldn't bear to close her eyes, to lose sight of him.

When, at last, they were joined, Nikki strove with him, against him, giving all of herself to the beauty of what she saw in his eyes, his face. And when the ecstasy peaked, her eyes closed to shut out the pleasure too great to bear. His face was still there behind her eyelids in a swirl of rainbow colors.

"Nicole . . . love." She opened her eyes again.

Their was a fierceness in his gaze, an intensity that

belied the soft smile that curved his lips. He lay there
a long moment, looking at her with that strange possessiveness in his face, then began to move away. She felt
a desperate need to hold him within her a few seconds
longer, to try to decipher that look before it changed.
She restrained him, pulling him back onto her, into her.

But the expression was gone. His smile was warm
and affectionate. He placed a soft kiss on her ravaged
mouth. With a glance beyond their little refuge, he said,
"The storm is almost over."

A need to keep this sweetness between them rushed
over Nikki. With a tiny smile she whispered, "Not
yet," and pulled his mouth back to hers.

Julian guided the cat into the boat shed alongside the
well-maintained, but ancient, run-about. He leaped onto
the dock and secured the boat, then reached back to
help Nikki with the beach towels and thermos.

The trip back had been accomplished in silence.
Nikki had felt too full, too complete to talk. She wanted
only to hug the warm afterglow to her as she watched
Julian work the sail. Words, she felt then, would have
been superfluous.

Now, as she accepted Julian's hand, she was acutely
conscious of her sea-snarled hair and the first stings of
a sunburn that seemed centered on her nose. "I'm a
mess," she muttered, looking down at her toes. "Come
with me to the guest house, and I'll give you some hot
cocoa while I slip into the shower."

His gaze went from her lips to her eyes, then back.
His eyes were smoky with things unspoken. "Fine,"
he said softly.

At her door Nikki found a note jammed in the crack.
She opened it and read:

If you two didn't drown, please be so good as to let me know.

K.

Smiling, Nikki handed the note to Julian and went inside. She padded across the oak parquet floor and put mugs of water into the microwave to heat. She took the dirty towels from Julian and went into the bathroom.

She came out a few moments later in a yellow terry kimono and draped a clean fluffy towel around Julian's bare shoulders. Kate's note, she noticed, was crumpled into a tight ball on the bar counter before him.

Julian caught her hand and pulled her to him. He restrained her when the timer on the microwave "dinged" and she would have pulled away. "We have to talk," he said.

"I know."

His hands slipped up the slender column of her throat to cradle her head as his mouth claimed hers in perfect communication. A wave of hot need possessed him as he slid his hands beneath the collar of her robe and eased it open, discovering that she wore nothing beneath. He moved back to gaze down at her lovely breasts, then drew her to him to feel them, soft and warm, against his naked chest.

"Love," Julian murmured against her hair. "I'm not normally an irresponsible man."

"I've never thought that you were." Nikki tilted her head back to look into his face. One of his dark brows rose sardonically.

"It's been five weeks since New Orleans. I came here because you should know by now whether or not you're pregnant."

"Pregnant?" The possibility had hardly occurred to her.

"Are you?" he rasped softly.

"No."

"You *would* tell me?"

"Yes."

"You wouldn't think it was more noble to try and handle it all yourself?"

"Of course not!" Nikki's faced burned red. "I'd never keep that kind of knowledge from you!"

"Good. Because we just took that chance again."

Nikki stared. The pleasant sense of well-being that she'd been enjoying suddenly grew tremulous. Julian's eyes were smoky and shadowed by something; almost a look of . . . pain? Whatever it was she couldn't comprehend it. Had he come back here only to assure himself she wasn't carrying his child?

"If I am pregnant, Julian, you will be the second to know." Nikki's forehead creased with the effort of remaining calm. She adjusted her robe. "Not that I would expect—" She turned away quickly to hide the tears that threatened to spill from her and pulled her sash tight. She straightened her shoulders, forced her face into an appearance of serenity. "I'd better call Kate. I'm sure she's very worried."

"I'll tell her," Julian said, his voice as harsh as the scrape of the stool as he pushed it back.

"Julian . . ." She turned back toward him to find cold eyes on her.

"I have to admit that I'm surprised by your affection for Kate," he snapped.

What did he mean by that? "She's—"

"A very special person," he interrupted. "I know. I love her dearly. But she's old, Nikki." His eyes probed hers and discomfort prickled her spine. "Aren't you afraid that you'll give her your friendship—your love—and she'll disappoint you by *dying*?" He seized her arms. His voice was harsh and mocking. "Tell me. Why are you willing to take a chance on a sure loss with Kate, when you won't take a chance on *me*?"

Nikki looked up into Julian's face, tense and dark with pain, and was shocked by it. She had always thought of him as indestructible; incapable of being truly hurt. "Oh, Julian," she moaned in sudden understanding. "Why didn't you ever tell me?"

"That I love you?" His silver eyes pierced her. "You didn't want to hear it." His harsh voice softened to a whisper. "You already knew."

Julian's expression softened and he stroked her cheek. Nikki opened her mouth again to speak.

"Shhh," he whispered. "Don't say it! Please." He continued, "If I were any kind of businessman, I'd have known when to cut my losses."

"I have to tell you—"

He stopped her words with gentle fingers. "No." He brushed her lips lightly with his and folded her against his chest. "Not now. If you said what I want to hear, it would only be because you feel sorry for me. No, don't deny it." A shuddering sigh racked him. "I have to go." He kissed her forehead and strode away.

"It was terrible of Julian to just disappear like that after dinner. But then as a boy he was always slipping away alone when something was eating at him," Kate said, glancing at Nikki as she worked behind the easel. *That one practically glowed*, she thought with a mental snort.

But Nikki would have denied that she glowed. She was still too puzzled by Julian's refusal to let her tell him how she felt.

"Kate, I'll bet you're a lousy fisherman. Your lures

make these giant splashes and they're phosphorescent orange and bristling with barbs.''

"That heavy-handed, huh?" Kate chuckled.

"Yup. Now stop talking so much or I'll have to add another purse line to your mouth." She focused her attention on the task before her again.

"Perverse child." Nikki hardly heard. All her concentration went into moving her brush from palette to canvas, palette to canvas. She had finished Kate's hands and face half an hour before. She was absorbed in adding a silken highlight to the muted drapes in the caftan. Like life and its many facets, the stripes turned and dipped and folded and curved in the most amazing detail, even undergoing a slight distortion when seen through the clear acrylic top of Kate's desk. But the dress didn't overpower the personality of the wearer. The woman on the canvas showed self-possession and a knowledge of self-worth. Her dark-rimmed glasses clasped in one hand, her head turned, and a sardonic sparkle in her dark eyes, she looked as if she'd just heard a supreme piece of impertinence and was about to deliver a devastating put down to its author.

Nikki relented when she saw how miserable her subject had become. "Okay, Kate. You can talk, but don't you dare move any of the rest of you."

"Good. I'd like to know if the subject came up."

Nikki had to think a long moment before she understood what Kate meant. "Marriage?"

"Yes."

"No."

Kate snorted. "I'm losing faith in that grandson of mine. I wonder if I should draw him a picture."

Nikki remembered Julian's incredible lovemaking as the rain drummed on the roof of the shack and smiled. "No-o-o. I don't think so, Kate." Her eyes met the older woman's and her smile deepened. "I think it might, maybe. The subject of marriage, I mean. Maybe."

Kate drew in a deep breath and let it out as a sigh. "That gives me the courage to sit for another three hours. Although I may not be able to walk afterward."

"No need. I'll be finished in another fifteen minutes if you'll just . . . hold *still*!"

"I can't help it. This is marvelous news! Tell me, exactly how long will it take the picture to dry? I'm anxious to send it to the framer's."

There's that look again, Nikki thought. Exactly like the cat who knows why its owner will find an empty birdcage at feeding time. "Oh, about a week," she answered. She changed brushes and started to finish the detail on the leather bound book.

"A week! Well, I suppose it'll have to do. I should like to have plenty of time to plan the unveiling party, anyway."

Nikki's brush faltered. "Unveiling party?"

Kate's black eyes sparkled. "Well, I was going to make it a surprise, but I don't intend to stretch my imagination to plan how to have you here and dressed properly at just the right hour."

Nikki cleaned her brush and put it away, not daring to speak. When the sudden rush of apprehension had subsided she told Kate, "You can get up now. I can finish the rest without you."

Kate did so, hiding a wince of pain as her stiff joints ached in protest. She came around behind the stool, put her hands on Nikki's shoulders and looked at the work in wonder. "It's special, dear," Kate said, swallowing a lump in her throat. Nikki patted the hand that had squeezed her left shoulder. "Bringing you here to paint my portrait is one of the nicest things Julian ever did for

212 / DIXIE DUBOIS

me—and would still have been if you'd never touched a brush.''

"Thank you, Kate." It had been a gift for them both, Nikki thought. In many different ways.

Looking back at Kate's portrait, Nikki knew it was the best work she'd ever done.

"Julian's still not available?" Nikki said into the telephone.

"He's out of the office. I don't think he's expected back this afternoon, Ms. Duval. Is there a message?" came the answer.

Kate walked through the doorway at that instant, carrying a crockery pot of African violets. "Did you get Julian yet?"

Nikki put her hand over the mouthpiece of the phone. "No. Just Svenson."

Kate rolled her eyes. "Atilla the Swede? Again?"

A throaty feminine chuckle coming over the phone told Nikki she hadn't quite covered the phone enough. "Give Mrs. Harrison my regards," the secretary said. "Is there a message?"

"No, thank you. Just . . . no." Nikki hung up the phone and glowered at it. Julian had called twice. She'd been out both times. And whenever she'd tried to get in touch with him . . .

"I know he's busy," she said, to no one in particular. Then her eye fell on something violet and red paisley—the edge of Kate's newest caftan.

"There are some colors that you wear," Nikki muttered. "And some colors that wear you. And some things which should be burned as a service to mankind. Gold lamé is the other one. Kate, that color combination positively blurs the vision!"

"What on earth are your babbling about?" the older

woman murmured as she gave her attention to a shelf of plants. Lifting one in a small ceramic pot, she said, "This one is supposed to be polka-dot."

Nikki blinked her eyes against a mental image of a caftan of swirling red-on-violet polka-dots. "I'm going to work," she declared, pushing back the sleeves of an old shirt of Julian's that she wore as a painting smock.

With Kate's portrait, her ability to paint had returned completely. Not with exactly the same vision that she had once had, but one deepened by age and life experience. As she painted she could lose herself for awhile, forget how much she missed Julian.

"Cheer up, dear. He'll be here for your party," Kate said, as if reading her thoughts.

"I know," Nikki sighed. But she really didn't. The more time passed, the less certain she was. "I know," she said more firmly, pushing back her doubts. She had been sure enough that she hadn't rented the beach house or accepted any commissions. It was no time to start doubting.

"Kate, I think I'll take the run-about and get those sketches of the shoreline that I've been wanting," Nikki said.

"That's a good idea," Kate said. "It'll keep your mind *off* things."

"Meaning it'll get me out from underfoot for your ladies' club meeting," Nikki said dryly.

"Exactly!" Kate snapped off a dead leaf. "Oh, by the way. I know it's slightly out of your way, but do try to ram the *Queen Mary* as you pass it. If I have to hear Laura Needham prosing on all afternoon about the *Dom Perignon* and *chateubriande* she's stocked up for their trip to Puerto Rico, you may just find her floating in the bay!"

*   *   *

The brush went from palette to canvas, palette to canvas. Nikki didn't have to think about skin tones or texture. She wasn't consciously thinking at all. Excitement rippled through her as she painted the small picture of Julian as she had seen him that first day in Grimes's office. She could see that smug, enticing look that spoke of his interest in her, and his sureness that she would be unable to resist. But there was also that quiet compassion beneath the surface.

That compassion had even overshadowed his cold, vindictive anger at Grimes's' swindle. Even with proof of the collusion, it had caused him to buy out Colomb Contractors just to save the jobs of the people who worked there. She understood that now. She knew the picture was exercise in self-indulgence. She needed Julian in her life—the thought still scared the hell out of her. And she hadn't heard from him since he'd gone away. Painting his picture kept her mind off how much she missed him and kept her doubts at bay.

Nikki swished the brush in the jar of turpentine and tapped it against her worktable. She decided to call it a day. She looked around with satisfaction at the paintings stacked around the walls of Kate's extra room that she used as a studio. Her favorite, besides the portrait of Kate, was an impressionist study of a common trick of light on the Sound in the late afternoon when both sea and sky paled to silvery blue and the line of the horizon was lost. A few of these she would sign. Most had been mere exercises. For the most part, she was pleased.

The sound of the telephone ringing made her start. When it stopped on the second ring, she knew that Kate had picked it up downstairs. "Silly heart," she muttered, hurrying to see. "It probably isn't him. Kate's phone rings a hundred times a day." Yeah, she thought. Kate's phone rings, but not the one in the guest house.

Nikki pushed the thought away. Julian had been busy. He was giving her time to make sure of what she wanted. He had tried to call, she just hadn't been in.

The sound of Kate's voice drifted up to her as she descended the stairs. "She's upstairs working. I can call her, Julian . . . oh, well all right, if that's what you want. But, Julian, I don't understand you sometimes." Kate grew impatient. "All right, if that's the way you want it. The party begins at eight o'clock tonight. I would have liked to see you sooner, but, if you can't . . . That will be fine, dear. Now what is the name of this woman you'll be bringing?"

Nikki froze just as she gained the door of Kate's study and some instinct for self-preservation made her take a step backward into the foyer. She didn't want to hear anymore. She couldn't stop listening.

Kate's voice took on an edge of serious concern. "Julian, shouldn't you tell Nikki? It's just not right to leave her without a word, then . . . All right, I won't say anything if you don't want me to, but—damn it!— I think you're wrong!" Kate hung up rather forcefully.

Nikki's eyes moved over the familiar patterns of the leaves of the dieffenbachia plant by the door as she held tightly to disbelief. Even if Julian had found someone he was more interested in—even if he had—he wasn't cruel. He'd never bring her here!

"Kate." Nikki forced her voice to sound natural. "Was that Julian you were talking with? He's bringing someone with him?"

Kate turned around in surprise. Her eyes were troubled as they searched Nikki's face. Then they dropped guiltily. "Yes. That was him. He'll be bringing . . .

an old friend from college. But there'll be no way he'll be able to get here before eight-thirty.''

"Kate, you should rest before this evening." Nikki smiled wanly. She patted Kate's hand distractedly. "I think I'll . . . go back to the guest house.''

"Damn Julian and his games," Kate said as she watched Nikki disappear down the walk.

FIFTEEN

The dark luxury sedan pulled up in the circular drive and stopped in front of the house. A young man in a red coat rushed forward. Kate, with her natural flair, had arranged for valet parking.

Julian tossed the keys to the young man and then opened the passenger door and helped a young woman out of the car. Her black hair was coiled low on her neck and she wore a sophisticated black dress beneath a white taffeta evening coat.

"I want to thank you again for coming tonight, Madeline," he said, looking down at her. "I see it as a personal favor."

"That's where you're wrong. It's part of my job. Besides it's good to get away from New York and the gallery, even if it is on business. And that one canvas you showed me was just enough to tantalize."

"Julian!" A very worried looking Kate met them at the door. She glanced at his companion with a nod. "Excuse me for being rude. I must talk to my grandson." With that, Kate pushed on the chest of his hand-pleated shirt, forcing him to take a step backward, then caught his arm and hauled him a few feet away.

Madeline Summers gave a mental shrug, then slung her white jacket more over her shoulders and followed the sounds of the party.

"Julian, it's Nikki!"

Something cool slipped along his spine. "Gram, calm down." Julian caught her hands in his. "It's not like you to get so upset. What's wrong?"

"She left in the boat this afternoon, and she's been gone for hours," she said, glancing out into the growing twilight. Only summer and daylight savings time had held the darkness back this long. "I called the sheriff's office an hour ago. They said they'd initiate a search. But it'll be dark soon, and there's such a large area . . ."

"Gram, did she say where she planned to go? Did she say anything?" he asked calmly.

"No. She didn't even say she was going. She just left."

He searched her face. "There's more, isn't there?"

"It's probably nothing. I'm sure it's nothing . . ."

"What?"

"Nikki came in right after I spoke with you this afternoon. She tried to hide it, but she looked upset. Julian, do you know anywhere she might have gone? What direction we should look?"

"You go back to the party." He led her to the door. "Everything will be fine, Gram." Looking up into Julian's calm self-assured features, she believed him.

After he'd seen his grandmother into the house, Julian sprinted away around the outside of the house to the private dock. He fought back a surge of panic.

"Nicole, you are an idiot!" Nikki said aloud, and kicked the engine hatch which housed a flat-head V-8 of 1952 vintage. The kick sounded loud in the quiet that was punctuated by the waves lapping against the classic boat's mahogany hull. She twisted the key in the ignition again. It produced only a series of clicks. The battery was too low to turn over the engine anymore.

"Damn!" she said, hitting the wheel with the flat of her palm. She would have liked to give herself a kick in the seat of the jeans—if that had been physically possible.

Why had she ignored the prime boating safety rule and gone off without telling someone where she was going? And at that in a boat without a radio! She deserved to be stuck out here while everyone was having a great time at the party. Julian would think her the biggest coward ever, hiding out for the unveiling. Or worse, that she'd pulled another disappearing act.

Nikki folded her arms on the steering wheel and rested her forehead against them.

It had been silly to run away to avoid seeing Julian with someone else. She'd come out here, to the island where they'd made love, to think. It hadn't taken long to find the answers.

Her art was back. And she wasn't afraid that it would vanish again. But that wasn't enough.

"You won't take a chance on me." Julian's words came back to her. He'd been right. Instead of trusting him, she'd been trying to stay in control of her emotions. The strange thing was that she did trust him. And why? She loved him! They couldn't have shared what they had if they hadn't loved each other. Julian had been right—she hadn't wanted to see that he loved her. She hadn't wanted to admit that she loved him—that he was more important to her than painting—or breathing.

She longed to go to him, now, to take away the pain

that had spawned those harsh words—to show him the true colors of her love.

But the damned engine wouldn't start.

Nikki lifted her head. She found that dusk had slipped into night. She slapped in annoyance at a mosquito, then noticed the drone of an engine in the distance. Some shrimpboat coming late to harbor. No! It was coming nearer.

With leaping excitement Nikki fumbled in the emergency kit for the flare gun. She forced herself to wait a few minutes until the lights of the boat got closer before she fired a flare. It made an orange arc in the darkness. The boat seemed to increase speed, but the craft was still far away.

"Thank goodness!" Nikki waved a few moments later as a spotlight on the boat found her. "Over here! Yes, here!" she shouted. She smothered a cry as the larger craft paused.

The boat was so big—too big. She realized that it would never be able to get into the shallow water close to the island where the run-about was anchored.

"Help! Oh, help!" she shouted as she tried to figure out how to get to the other boat. She was answered by a splash. A dark form cut through the pool of light shed on the water by the spotlight. Nikki sat down abruptly as he hauled himself a board.

"Nikki! My God, are you all right?" Julian was kneeling before her, touching her face with dripping hands.

"Julian? Of course, I'm all right!"

"Your sure?" As his thumbs stroked her prominent cheekbones his eyes inspected every inch of her face, then he pulled back to look over the rest of her. "When you called for help, I thought . . ."

"Oh, Julian! I'm sorry. I just couldn't figure out how to get to your boat! I didn't have a paddle."

Julian saw from her rueful smile that what she said was true. She was all right. He relaxed with a deep sigh.

"Thank God you're okay. When Kate said that you'd been gone for hours, I panicked."

"I can tell." Nikki smoothed water from his forehead and cheeks, then moved to his throat. "You're still wearing your tie." She tugged it loose and unfastened the collar. Her eyes caressed his, glorying in all the love and caring she found in them. "Julian, I love you."

He wrapped her in a fierce embrace. "Oh, God! I've waited so long, hoping to hear you say that! Nikki why did you leave? You knew I'd be there for the unveiling."

Nikki looked down, embarrassed. With his finger beneath her chin, Julian tilted her head back up, forcing her to meet his eyes. "I overheard Kate on the phone and I thought that you'd given up on me and were bringing someone else. I didn't want to be there when you came.

"But as soon as I got out here I realized how stupid that assumption was and how much I really trusted you. Besides, I realized that you're too classy a guy to parade a new love interest at my party—even if you had given up on me. But before I could get back, the damn boat broke." Her voice dropped to a whisper.

"I really do trust you, Julian. I didn't want to. It's just that you meant so much to me. It frightened me. It still does."

"It's scary as hell. I know. That's how much I love you. But now I know it'll be all right." His mouth sought hers. Nikki tilted her head back to receive the fire of his kiss. Reaction shivered through her, as she suspected it always would. "Julian," she gasped at length. "You're getting me sopping wet. We have to get to the other boat to dry off and call Kate to let her know that we're okay." She turned to peer across the water at the other craft. "What *is* that thing, anyway?"

Julian looked guiltily toward the spotlight of the boat swinging at anchor. "I . . . When Kate told me that you were missing, all I could think of was getting out here—hoping that this was where you'd come. I'm afraid I, uh, borrowed it from Kate's neighbors."

"Not the *Queen Mary*!" Nikki gasped, then laughed. Pulling back within the circle of his arms, she began undoing shirt studs.

"What are you doing, love?" Julian asked, his heart doubling its tempo as her clever fingers exposed his chest.

Nikki took the time to place a warm kiss on his breastbone before answering. "We have to swim over there and let Kate know we're okay. Then, Archer," she said ominously, "I intend to make love to you until you agree to marry me."

Julian's eyes glowed silver in the half-light. "In that case, I should warn you, my love, since the galley on that boat appeared to be very well stocked, I think I can hold out for several days."

SHARE THE FUN . . .
SHARE YOUR NEW-FOUND TREASURE!!

You don't want to let your new book out of your sight? That's okay. Your friends can get their own. Order below.

No. 37 ROSES by Caitlin Randall
K.C. and Brett join forces to find who is stealing Brett's designs. But who will help them both when they find their hearts are stolen too?

No. 38 HEARTS COLLIDE by Ann Patrick
Matthew knew he was in trouble when he crashed into Paula's car but he never dreamed it would be this much trouble!

No. 39 QUINN'S INHERITANCE by Judi Lind
Quinn and Gabe find they are to share in a fortune. What they find is that they share much, much more—and it's priceless!

No. 40 CATCH A RISING STAR by Laura Phillips
Fame and fortune are great but Justin finds they are not enough. Beth, a red-haired, green-eyed bundle of independence, is his greatest treasure.

No. 41 SPIDER'S WEB by Allie Jordan
Silvia's quiet life explodes when Fletcher shows up on her doorstep.

No. 42 TRUE COLORS by Dixie DuBois
Julian helps Nikki find herself again but will she have room for him?

No. 43 DUET by Patricia Collinge
Two parts of a puzzle, Adam & Marina glue their lives together with love.

No. 44 DEADLY COINCIDENCE by Denise Richards
J.D.'s instincts tell him he's not wrong; Laurie's heart says trust him.
